A Goode Girls Romance

Dancing With Danger

KERRIGAN BYRNE

OLIVER HEBER BOOKS

0 9 8 7 6 5 4 3 2 1

Cover by: Midnight Muse Designs

Published by Oliver Heber Books

CHAPTER 1

LONDON, 1881

*A*n incomparable idiot.

It was the only description for the man blocking Mercy Goode from the murder scene *she'd* discovered her own self.

And yet he had the *audacity* to sneer down at her in that condescending way menial men did when granted a little bit of authority. His shiny badge declared him Constable M. Jenkins. A tall but scrawny bit of bones scraped together between comically overgrown muttonchops.

"If you don't vacate the premises now, I'll see you sleeping behind bars tonight, and make no mistake about that." He narrowed beady eyes and loomed in an attempt to intimidate her.

Mercy glared right back. Since she was entirely too short for a proper loom, she bared her teeth to do him one better in the foul expression department.

An errant bee had more capacity to terrify her than this blighter with his ridiculous feathery mustache. From the moment he'd arrived, he'd tried to get rid of her, and *that* she would not abide.

"See here!" Mercy poked him in the chest. "*I'm* the one who found the body thus murdered and sent for

Scotland Yard. Therefore, I'm a valuable witness at best and a possible suspect at the very least. If you advise me to leave before a detective inspector arrives, he'll be furious. You could lose your position, which..." She trailed off, scanning the man up and down for any possible signs of capability. "If you want my opinion, might do both you and the London Metropolitan Police a favor."

The slack-jawed halfwit blinked in mute amazement, his dull brain taking an inordinate amount of time to process her statement.

Mercy used his dumbstruck torpor to sweep around him and slide into the stately, feminine solarium where the corpse sat propped in a high-backed burgundy velvet chair.

Poor Mathilde.

Swallowing a lump of regret so large it threatened to choke her, Mercy's hands curled into fists. Mathilde had known she was in danger. They'd discussed it at length when the scandalous socialite—bruised, battered, and quite drunk—had come seeking shelter at the Duchess of Trenwyth's Lady's Aid Society. The Duchess, along with Mercy's twin, Felicity, had hatched a plan to secretly smuggle the woman out of the country as soon as humanly possible.

Evidently, not soon enough.

If only they had made other arrangements.

If only Mercy had skipped her weekly appointment last evening and insisted on squiring Mathilde away under the cover of night, instead of allowing the sweet —but unreliable—woman to decide upon the circumstances.

When she wanted to dissolve into frustrated tears, Mercy only allowed herself to indulge in a hitch of labored breath before she bit into the flesh of her cheek. It was imperative she contain herself. She could not show weakness.

Not here.

Not in front of a man who would whip her with it. Who would make her wait somewhere else until she controlled her "feminine hysterics."

The very idea was intolerable.

"I'm so sorry I failed you," she whispered to the unnaturally still body. Her fingers itched to brush back one errant lock of what was otherwise a perfect brunette coiffure.

Mathilde had been a beautiful woman in the prime of her thirties. Scandalous, sultry, and... scared.

They'd only ever met in person but thrice. And yet, Mercy felt this tragedy as if a dear friend had passed.

"I vow I will not rest until they find who did this to you," she whispered.

At those words, a strange, feverish chill washed down her spine and prickled along her nerve endings. She was suddenly bathed in awareness of someone nearby.

Watching.

Glancing about, she only found Jenkins, apparently roused from his stupefied confusion at her feint around his blockade.

Perhaps it was time for her to rethink her position regarding ghosts.

She'd been categorically opposed to the idea of the supernatural in almost every respect.

Until now.

Certainly Jenkins didn't carry such an aura of malice.

Even though she'd made him cross.

"Oi!" He stormed into the room after her, his expression morphing from one of surprise to suspicion. "The detective inspector isn't but a moment away, so don't you dare touch anything."

"I know better than to disturb a murder scene," Mercy announced with a droll sniff.

"What makes you reckon she was murdered?" he asked, eyeing her with rank skepticism. "The lady could have very well died in her sleep. You know something you're not telling?"

Despite her distress and remorse, Mercy felt a surge of relish at being able to finally trot her extensive knowledge on the matters of murder in the presence of an arrogant dolt.

"Prepare your notepad, dear Constable, and I shall elucidate." She pinned her hands behind her back in a regimental posture. One her brilliant brothers-in-law often adopted when lecturing her about being more judicious.

Not that such homilies were effectual in her case.

But the men in her family appeared especially important and erudite while standing thusly, and even though she didn't usually listen, it was certain that most people who were unacquainted with their soft hearts and darkest secrets would be inclined to do so.

"Do you see the slight edema there at her neck?" She motioned to the open throat of Mathilde's high-necked gown, where the once-porcelain skin was now tinged a blue-grey. "This suggests asphyxiation, but there are no ligature marks, nor is there bruising." She bent closer, inspecting the wound. "But a distressing bit of an interruption in the cords of her muscle, just there, leads me to believe that when your coroner arrives, he'll find that her neck has been quite broken."

Mercy exhaled a shaking breath, grasping onto her composure with both hands. If this dullard could keep his wits about him when faced with such a tragedy, then she was equally determined to.

"She wouldn't have died instantly." Her throat rasped over traitorous emotion. "Likely, she'd have

4

been paralyzed, but able to talk and scream until the pressure crushed her trachea." Her fingers reached for her own neck in sympathy, her bones heavy with guilt and her heart surging with an ardent vow to retaliate. "Her name was Mathilde Archambeau. That's A-R-C-H —" She glanced over at Jenkins. "Why are you not writing this down?"

"Because we know exactly who this woman is," said a stolid voice from the doorway. "And we have already surmised who is responsible for her death."

Mercy whirled to find an average, if incredibly sturdy, man in a billycock hat and matching grey morning suit. He strode into the solarium with his coat lackadaisically draped over one arm. A square chin framed a nose that could have been unflatteringly likened to a potato. Eyes spaced too close together gleamed with improper interest as he conducted a thorough and disrespectful examination of Mercy's person.

He was at least fifteen years her senior and wore a wedding band on his left finger.

Marriage didn't stop men from ogling her, Mercy had found. Most possessed a weakness for a young slim woman with pale ringlets and a passably attractive face.

That was all they saw when they looked at her with the same desire she witnessed now. Her smooth, unblemished youth. Her diminutive shape and sparkling blue eyes.

She could disarm just about anyone with her winsome charms.

Until she opened her mouth.

Then their desire melted into anything from dismay to disgust.

As Mercy's father often said, she'd make a perfect wife, if only someone could relieve her of her wits and her willfulness.

5

Or at least her tongue.

Her charms, as it happened, were only skin-deep.

Ah well, c'est la vie.

Fingers the size of breakfast sausages curled around her gloved hands as the newcomer bowed over her knuckles. "I'm Detective Inspector Martin Trout, at your service, Miss..."

Trout. A more apropos surname was never given.

"You know who did this?" Mercy plucked her hand away, blithely stepping around his subtle press for an introduction. "You know who murdered Mathilde?"

"That's a relief. I was beginning to think it was *her*." Constable Jenkins gestured toward Mercy, his brass buttons catching on the afternoon light streaming in through the windows from the back gardens.

One such window, Mercy noted, was open.

In February?

When even the fire blazing in the hearth wasn't enough to ward off the moist chill in the room.

"Don't be ridiculous, Jenkins," Detective Inspector Trout said, sidling closer to Mercy. "Our division is very familiar with this household. Mrs. Archambeau was unquestionably killed by her ham-fisted husband, Gregoire."

Mercy deflated instantly. So much for the police being any help. "No, Detective Inspector, that is where you are wrong. It had to have been someone else."

"Wrong?" The man echoed the word as if he'd never heard it before as shadows passed over his ruddy features.

Mercy nodded. "Mathilde and I had someone follow Gregoire onto a ferry to France where he was to conduct business for a week at least. You see, while he was away, she was going to leave him, due to the aforementioned mistreatment of her." At this, Mercy's brows drew together as she speared the man with her most imperious glare. "Which begs the question, Detective Inspector Trout, if you were aware that Mr. Archambeau was a cruel man, why didn't you arrest him or at least take measures to keep poor Mathilde safe?"

Ah, there it was. The dulling of his desire.

All semblance of approbation drained from Trout's murky eyes, replaced by instant antipathy. "Mathilde Archambeau is a notorious drunkard and recently made a cuckold of her husband on a number of occasions," he informed her stiffly.

"Yes," Mercy clipped, "Mathilde admitted to me that she drank, among other things, to dull the anxiety and misery of living with such a man as Mr. Archambeau..." Stalling, she also recalled the rapturous expression on the woman's features when she'd confided that she'd taken a lover recently. One who'd coaxed such pleasure from her body, she'd become addicted to that, as well.

If only Mercy hadn't been too embarrassed—and too stimulated—to ask the man's name.

For, surely, *he* was a suspect.

"Certainly, Mathilde's indiscretions didn't warrant violence against her. Indeed, she didn't deserve this terrible fate," she said.

"I don't know about that." Trout gave a tight, one-shouldered shrug and twisted his lips into something acerbic and ugly as he glanced down at the departed. "Were I to catch my missus with anyone, I don't imagine the outcome would be much different. She'd be lucky to escape with a sound hiding, and *he'd* be certain to end up in the Thames."

This, from a man who'd undressed her with his eyes, only moments before.

Mercy decided to take a different approach.

It was that or lose her temper.

"Look over here." She hurried to the window and swiped at the ledge, the silk of her white glove coming away dirty with mud from the garden. "I entered the Archambeau household through the front door, as would Gregoire, if he'd come home early. Someone very obviously climbed in this window recently. Someone strong and limber, to have scaled up to the third-floor terrace in last night's rain. Strong enough to say... snap a woman's neck with his bare hands." She moved the drapes out of the way, uncovering one large footprint in the arabesque carpet. "I deduce that if you find the man who wears a military Brogan boot with such a definitive heel, you'll find Mathilde's murderer."

She couldn't say that she expected an ovation or anything, but the grim consternation on both the lawmen's faces threatened to steal some of the wind from her sails. "Confirm Gregoire's absence from the country if you must—no one would fault you for being thorough—but also it's your duty to examine and investigate any other evidence, and this is certainly compelling." She looked at Trout pointedly. "Do you happen to know the name of her lover? Maybe he—"

Trout moved with astonishing speed for a man of his girth and was in front of her in an instant. Those large sausage fingers of his spanned her wrist in a bruising grip and yanked her away from the window. "Time for you to leave."

"Unhand me, sir!" Mercy demanded.

He dragged her toward the door, speaking through clenched teeth. "Regardless of her supposed wealth, Mathilde Archambeau was a degenerate who associated with students, theater folk, socialists, and suffragists. Her husband is little better. I do not know to which group you belong, but I'll tell you this... you'll be hard-pressed to find a detective who will spend extra precious time and energy on behalf of a drunken immigrant slag. Her death means there is one less *nasty* woman in my borough—"

Mercy's hand connected with the detective's cheek before she realized she'd meant to slap him. Her palm stung, even beneath her glove, and she'd barely time to close her fingers around it before her blow was answered with a backhand to the jaw.

The force was such that her neck gave an audible crack when it wrenched to the side. She would rather have died than allow a cry to escape, but the pain was so acute, so startling, she couldn't hold in the whimper.

Jenkins stepped toward them. The frown of concern twisting his mustache blurred as hot, unwanted tears muddled Mercy's vision.

"Inspector, is such brutality necessary—"

"Shut up, Jenkins, and get me the shackles. I'm arresting this harpy for accosting an officer of—"

The sound of splintering wood froze all in the room into a momentary tableau of shock as the door on the far wall shattered beneath an overwhelming force.

Mercy's pulse slammed in her veins as recognition seized her with a queer and instantaneous paralysis.

The last—well, the only—time she'd seen the newcomer, his gait had been lazy and arrogant. His movements loose-limbed and careless, as if he'd conquer the world when he bothered to get around to it.

He had made it abundantly clear to her in the past that he did nothing lest it pleased him.

And what he took pleasure in at this moment, was violence.

All semblance of charm and leisure had been replaced by a body coiled with the tension of steel cables and grey eyes glinting with all the lethality of gunmetal.

He was across the room in a blink, lunging like a viper.

He struck. Struck again.

Blood flew and bone crunched.

Suddenly, Trout was no longer grasping her but

crumpled in a moaning puddle at her feet.

When Jenkins reached for his cudgel, the interloper only had to whirl and point a long finger in his direction to cause the lawman anxious hesitation. "If you raise that weapon against me, *mon ami*, I swear in front of God—and this beautiful woman—that I will take it and deliver the most humiliating beating you've ever received."

His voice like a saber, smooth and wickedly sharp, was tinged with the barest hint of a French accent. It slid into her ear with that same vague sensation of malevolence she'd experienced only moments ago, raising every hair on her body.

Some primitive instinct roared to life in his presence, one that warned her of imminent peril.

"The last man who raised a weapon against me...will never walk again." He stood with his back to her, squared against the indecisive constable. Lean muscle flexed rigid beneath his exquisitely tailored suit as vibrations of aggression and intimidation rolled off his wide shoulders in waves and stole whatever courage poor Jenkins possessed.

The policeman returned trembling fingers to his sides as he, no doubt, recognized how close he stood to death.

Because the man in front of him was possessed of one of the most identifiable names in the empire.

A notorious libertine.

A flagrant and lawless fortune hunter.

A gangster bequeathed with all the masculine beauty of Eros himself.

He turned back to her, brushing an errant ebony forelock of hair out of his eyes to aid in his unrepentant assessment.

What Mercy read in his gaze stupefied her further.

Where before there had been intellect, charisma,

and cunning, only ferocity resided now. Ferocity and...something that looked confoundingly like concern.

His evaluation was a tangible thing. It caressed her in places she'd given no man license to touch.

Least of all him.

His scan of her body started at the hem of her dress and left no part of her untouched until he met her eyes.

And then, right in front of her, the ferocity dissipated, replaced by that signature insouciance he was so famous for.

It was said he'd smile like a Cheshire cat whilst disemboweling his enemies.

Mercy didn't doubt it in the least.

He lifted his knuckles to brush against her still-smarting cheek, and she flinched away.

Not because she feared him—

But because she wasn't ready to find out what the sensation of his touch would do to her. When his very presence set her nerves alight with such volatile, visceral thrums of awareness, how could she bear the pressure of his skin?

He obviously misinterpreted her retreat as a muscle flexed in his jaw. "I will relieve him of the hand he struck you with, *mademoiselle.*"

He said this as if offering to shine her shoe.

A siren broke the moment as the thunder of horse hooves clattered into the cobbled courtyard. Voices shouted and the very rafters shook with the force of a veritable army of police.

The arrival of his comrades injected the sputtering constable with fresh nerve.

"No one will believe this," Jenkins marveled. "I'll be the man who arrested *the* Raphael Sauvageau, Lord of the Fauves, and hanged him for murder.

11

*M*ercy had often been described as fearless. Indeed, she did little to disavow people of the notion. In her home, fear was used by her authoritarian parents to coerce and control. She witnessed how it plagued Felicity, her twin. How it granted her domineering father power over people he had no right to possess.

And so, she'd decided from a very young age that she would fear as little as possible and therefore maintain as much power as she could.

Oddly enough, an ironic phobia had developed in the wake of her declaration of personal sovereignty.

She couldn't stand to be caged.

In fact, the confines of the prisoner transport wagon made her fingers curl with the need to claw at the locks, the walls, the very flesh that immured her soul to her body.

The shiver that had previously run through her had now become a quake so intense, her bones threatened to rattle together.

Though the iron and wood interior of their cage was intolerably frigid, a sheen of sweat perceptibly bloomed at her hairline and some of it gathered to trickle between her breasts. The sway of the coach on dubious springs felt to her like a rowboat on the open ocean during a sea gale.

It was making her green at the gills.

Well, if her breakfast were to make a reappearance, she'd be certain to direct it at the shackled man taking up more than his share of space, not to mention entirely too much of the fetid air.

She refused to acknowledge Raphael Sauvageau as she lunged at the door, kicking out at it with all her might. The irons securing her wrists in front of her were attached to a bar above the long bench by a chain that set her teeth on edge with the most grating rattle.

As the carriage lurched over a bump, the chains were the only reason she didn't end up on the floor in a heap of petticoats and sprawling limbs.

Mercy hadn't gone easily into confinement. She'd writhed and scratched and spit like an angry tomcat being forced into a bath. It'd taken four constables to subdue her.

Behind her, the damnable gangster had sauntered toward his imprisonment as if he were on a lazy stroll, looking so much like he preferred his hands to be manacled behind him so he didn't have to hold them there on his own.

His calm was patently infuriating. And if she were speaking to him at the moment, she'd make certain he knew it.

"Let me out, you knob-headed ignoramus!" she shouted through the bars, gripping them and shaking, as if it would do any good. "It shouldn't be a crime to slap a man for being a discourteous toad, especially when he gave as good as he got!"

She ignored a sound emanating from the man locked inside with her, unable to tell if it was mirth or wrath.

The uniformed officers around Mathilde's tidy row house disappeared as the conveyance rounded a corner.

In one final fit of pique, Mercy slammed her palm against the door with a satisfying clang before heaving herself onto the bench in a huff.

"I can't be here," she said to no one. Particularly *not* to the only other occupant of the coach. "My father is a baron and a commissioner, and my brother-in-law is the Chief Inspector at Scotland Yard. I'll never hear the end of it." She tugged at her tight manacles, twisting her slim wrists this way and that. "Oh, blast and bloody bother!"

This time, the rumble of amusement was unmistakable, drawing her notice.

"Really, I must beg you to refrain from saying such things," Raphael Sauvageau intoned in a voice that threatened to curl her toes.

He lazed on the bench across from her as if it were as comfortable as a throne, legs sprawled open at the knees and expensive jacket undone. The threads of his trousers molded to long, powerful thighs, calling attention to an indecent bulge at their apex.

"I'll say what I like, you—you—" If she wasn't doing her best to avoid looking at it—at *him*—she would surely have delivered a most clever and scathing remark.

"Do not misunderstand me, *mon chaton*, I have no wish to censure you. It is only that I find your attempts at profanity relentlessly adorable and distracting. It is torture to be unable to do anything about it." Beneath his charcoal suit, he lifted a helpless shoulder made no less broad for the captivity of his arms behind his back.

"The only thing you can do is to sod right off," she snipped. "They're going to put you to death, how can you be so calm?"

That Gallic shrug again. "I have many reasons not to

14

panic, not the least of which is that I don't want to give them the satisfaction of knowing they ruffled my feathers." He raised one dark, expressive eyebrow at her.

Mercy felt her frown turn into a scowl. Every person in a five-city-block radius categorically understood the current state of her feathers. They hadn't been merely ruffled. But plucked.

Fit to be tied, she was.

Drat.

Mercy sagged back and let her head fall against the wall, squeezing her eyes shut.

She didn't want to look at him.

What was he about calling her adorable? Had he meant it as a slight? A condescending jab at her youth? She was only all of twenty, but she was well educated. Well read.

Not to mention...one just didn't go around calling people adorable, did one? Not unless they were your nine-year-old niece or something equally perturbing.

She was a *woman*.

And some part of her wanted him to know that. To acknowledge it.

Raphael Sauvageau was pure, unmitigated male. His voice deep. His manner predatory. His gaze unapologetically lustful.

When he spoke, his voice purred against her skin.

And yet, he could seduce a woman without saying a word. Make her aware of all the deep, empty places she ignored.

He was wickedly, no, *ruthlessly* attractive. Roguish and virile with sharp bones that cut a portrait of indolent cruelty.

That was why she refused to open her eyes, because sometimes, looking at him made her brain turn to a puddle of useless, feminine liquid that threatened to leak out her ears, leaving her with no wits at all.

With no logic. No reason to resist...

Regardless of her attempt to ignore him, she could feel his eyes upon her like the gaze of some ancient divinity. Pulling at her sinew and bone. Sucking at her veins as if he could drink her in.

What *was* he?

How many women were charred in the combustible heat of such a gaze?

She didn't want to know.

Furthermore, she refused to be one of them.

Their first and only previous encounter had been the summer before. She'd gone with her eldest sister, Honoria—whom they called Nora—and Felicity in search of a missing fortune to save the man Nora had loved her entire life.

When they'd found the fortune in gold, they'd also found Raphael Sauvageau, the half-Monégasque, half-English leader of the fearsome Fauves—a French word meaning "wild beasts." He and his brother, Gabriel, laid claim to the gold that had been stolen by Nora's criminally atrocious first husband, the Viscount Woodhaven.

Their meeting had been fraught with intensity and the suggestion of threat.

Mercy and Raphael had sparred verbally, and she'd gone away with the feeling that he'd enjoyed it.

Or perhaps that she had.

Mercy's brothers-in-law, Chief Inspector Carlton Morley and Dr. Titus Conleith, had found out and come for the sisters, confronting the Sauvageau brothers.

Instead of a war breaking out between the men, Raphael and Gabriel had relinquished their gold to Titus and Honoria, which had been a substantial amount, with a promise to return for some mysterious future medical procedure.

According to Titus, he'd not heard from the Sauvageau brothers in the months since.

None of them had.

And yet, the rogue had often intruded, unbidden and unwanted, into Mercy's thoughts. She'd remember how he looked in the dim light of the lone lantern the night they'd met. All lean muscle and vibrating intimidation subdued by a veneer of cunning, charisma and undeniable intelligence.

He lurked always in the periphery of her silent moments. Like a serpent in the shadows, deceptively calm, coiled to strike.

He was an invasion. A trespasser. And he didn't even know it.

Or maybe he did.

Maybe...he'd done it on purpose. Some sort of serpentine mesmerism that had nothing to do with her unruly thoughts and desires, and everything to do with his villainy.

Yes, that must be it.

The fault was his, obviously.

Had he worked the same sort of magic on Mathilde?

That thought sobered her enough to redirect her panic into rage.

"May the devil fetch you if you hurt Mathilde." Though her eyes remained closed, she injected as much virulence into her words as she could summon.

"He'll fetch me regardless, but I... cared for her."

Despite herself, the veracity in his voice drew Mercy's lids open so she could study him for other signs of deceit.

His expression was drawn and serious.

Lethally so.

Daylight slanted in through the bars, making his eyes glint like polished steel. Motes of dust frenzied in his atmosphere as if drawing energy from the electric force of his presence. A thin ring of gold glinted in his left ear, and sharp cheekbones underscored an arrogant brow.

He'd look stern but for his mouth, which was not so severe. It bowed with a fullness she might have called feminine if the rest of his face wasn't so brutally cast.

Mercy hadn't realized she'd been staring at his lips, gripped with a queer sort of fascination, until they parted and he spoke.

"You were quite impressive back there."

"What?" Mercy shook her head dumbly. Had he just complimented her? Had they just been through the same scene? She'd never been less impressed with herself in her entire life.

Would that she could have been like him. Smooth and unaffected. Infuriatingly self-assured.

And yet...he'd only been that way after breaking the nose of the officer that had struck her, and possibly his jaw.

Lord but she'd never seen a man move like that before.

"I listened to your deductions," he explained.

"From where you were hiding in the closet?" she quipped, rather unwisely.

Something flickered in his eyes, and yet again she was left to guess if she'd angered or amused him.

"From where I was hiding in the closet," he said with a droll sigh as he shifted, seeming to find a more comfortable position for his bound hands. "You're obviously cleverer than the detectives. How do you know so much about murder scenes?"

Mercy warned herself not to preen. She stomped on the lush warmth threatening to spread from her chest at his encouragement, and thrust her nose in the air, perhaps a little too high. "I am one of only three female members of the Detective Eddard Sharpe Society of

Homicidal Mystery Analysis. As penned by the noted novelist J. Francis Morgan, whom I suspect is a woman."

"Why do you suspect that?" His lip twitched, as if he also battled to suppress his own expression.

"Because men tend to write female characters terribly, don't they? But J. Francis Morgan is a master of character and often, the mystery is even solved by a woman rather than Detective Sharpe. His heroines are not needlessly weak or stupid or simpering. They're strong. Dangerous. Powerful. Sometimes even villainous and complicated. That is good literature, I say. Because it's true to life."

He'd ceased fighting his smile and allowed his lip to quirk up in a half-smile as he regarded her from beneath his dark brow. "Mathilde's murderer now has one more person they'd do well to fear in you."

She leveled him a sour look. "Does that mean you fear me?"

He tilted toward her. Suddenly—distressingly—grave. "You terrify me, Mercy Goode."

She had to swallow twice before she could deliver her question without sounding as breathless as she felt.

"Did you do it?" She leaned forward, bracing her elbows on her knees as she examined his features thoroughly. "Did you kill Mathilde Archambeau?"

"No." He looked her in the eye as he said this. Unblinking. Unwavering. "She was dead when I arrived."

The ache in his voice tugged at her and, she was ashamed to admit, uncoiled something complicated from around her guts. Something dark and unfamiliar.

Surely not jealousy.

Not for a dead woman.

Not because of a man like him.

"Why didn't you call for the police, then?" she demanded.

He flexed his shackled arms, leveling her a droll look of his own. "I'm one of the most wanted men in the empire."

Berating her own stupidity, she winced, causing the welt on her cheek where she'd been struck to throb. Testing the wound gingerly, she sighed, grateful her fingers were cold against the sore, swelling flesh.

"What were you doing there in the first place?" she queried impatiently.

He didn't answer.

Instead, his gaze affixed on the spot where her fingers explored her own cheek. Every twitch of discomfort she made seemed to turn his eyes a darker shade of grey, as if a storm gathered within them.

"I will break every bone below that man's elbow for the pain he caused you." Shards of gravel paved a voice that had only just been smooth as silk.

"I abhor violence," Mercy lied, if only to condemn him.

If only to escape the very visceral vibrations that shimmered through her at the ferocity in his tone.

She drew her fingers from her face and folded them as primly in her lap as her manacles would allow.

He snorted with disbelief. "Is that why you read the macabre mysteries of Detective Eddard Sharpe? They are always deliciously brutal. Which is your favorite?"

She set her jaw stubbornly against a little thrill at the idea of discussing the books with him, but refused to be drawn in. He was a criminal and a condemned man.

A foe. Not a friend.

"I shouldn't think a man such as yourself took the time to read...or even knew how." She was acting the spoiled baron's daughter, but she thought it might make that illumination behind his gaze dull. That blaze of interest. The heat that hadn't waned during their conversation, but grew in strength and brilliance.

He simply stared at her expectantly until she found herself blurting, "My favorite is *The Legacy of Lord Lennox.*"

His eyebrow lifted again. "If I'm not mistaken, it's the most violent of the series. A man gets sawed into pieces and his bits are delivered to his family members. One of whom is the murderer."

"That's different," she huffed, refusing to be impressed. Refusing to picture the man in front of her lazing about some chaise longue, his limbs slack and his shirt undone as his eyes traced rows of delectable words.

Did he nibble at his cheek as he read? Or perhaps thread those elegant fingers through his hair...

She snorted at her own absurdity. "Fiction. Entertainment safely contained in the jacket of a book."

"In my experience, reality is ever so much more fantastic than fiction. And nothing is so dangerous as the written word. It is how power is usurped and ideas are spread. Literature is the most dangerous weapon a man can use. After all, it has been written that the pen is mightier than—"

"Are you afraid of the noose?" she interrupted him abruptly, for if he finished quoting Edward Bulwer-Lytton, she might do something ridiculous.

Like kiss him.

He shocked her with that effortless rumble she was coming to recognize as his chuckle. "I'm not going to hang, *mon chaton.*"

"Stop calling me that," she spat. "If you are half of what they say you are, if you've committed half the crimes you've been credited with, I don't see how you can escape execution."

Raphael leaned forward, the light across his eyes

following the shape of his brow, gleaming off the ebony of his hair and then settling on his shoulders like Apollo's own mantle as he brought their faces flush.

Mercy had to force herself not to lean back.

Somehow that felt like a retreat.

"What things do they say I am?" he murmured.

She ticked them off on her fingers as she answered around a dry tongue, pretending his proximity didn't distress her. "A hedonist. A libertine. A profligate. Scoundrel. Gangster."

"Ah, for once, *they* are right," he admitted wryly.

"A murderer?"

Cool air kissed her neck, but what caused her to shiver was the tantalizing heat of his breath as he bent even closer. "I have helped men to the next world, *mon chaton*. But I've never hurt a woman. I did not kill your friend."

"Then I ask you again. What were you doing there? Were you Mathilde's lover?"

A muted clang caused them both to jump, and Mercy let out a little cry of surprise as the back of the carriage dipped slightly.

She couldn't say if it was the movement or her own instinct that shifted her body closer to his warmth.

To his strength.

Even though he smirked down at her with no little amount of masculine smugness, his gaze searched hers for something.

For permission?

An inner voice warned her that if she opened her mouth, it would be granted.

She lunged away then, scooting to the far edge of the bench in time for the door to swing open.

While they were still moving?

A mountain of a man in a dark coat and a hood slid inside and closed the door behind him. He turned his head toward her, but in the dim coach, she couldn't make out anything that resembled a face.

Only a dark abyss was visible in the oval of shadow left by his low hood and his collar.

He stared at her from the darkness, though.

Nay, examined her like one might scrutinize an insect before crushing it beneath his shoe.

With wicked claws he scored that instinct that lived in every human. The one that screamed a warning into her soul that she was not safe.

Her bones veritably crawled beneath her skin to escape him.

If Raphael was dangerous, this man was...well, he defied description.

"What took you so long, Gabriel?" Raphael hissed. "Ten minutes more and it would have been too late."

Raphael's brother said nothing. He studied her for the space of two more discomfiting blinks and then gave her his massive back, bending toward his brother.

She'd been dismissed.

It would have offended her, were she not so relieved. It was as if she'd disappointed him, somehow.

As if he'd been looking for someone else.

He produced thin metal instruments from his coat and deftly—for a man with hands as large as his—went to work at the lock on his brother's manacles.

Mercy could count on one hand the times she'd been rendered speechless.

Gabriel Sauvageau had picked the padlock of a police vehicle and slid inside *while it was moving* without raising the alarm or even alerting the drivers.

How was this done?

While he worked to free his brother, he muttered in barely perceptible French, his voice a rasping whisper that hinted at a baritone as dark, deep, and smooth as moonlight over marble.

The very devil might have a voice like that.

Mercy had always been a terrible student. She wiggled too much, her brain pinging from one thing to the next until so many of her thoughts threatened to tumble everywhere like a litter of unruly puppies.

But she'd retained a rudimentary understanding of French.

And if she wasn't mistaken, Gabriel had said something to the effect that they'd rescheduled a meeting at the zoo to the following Wednesday at...three o'clock?

"You're being unspeakably rude," she admonished them, hoping to hide that she comprehended their conversation.

Well... sort of comprehended it.

Raphael had the decency to look chagrined. "In this case, I must beg your forgiveness, *mon chaton*, as my brother speaks very little English."

"Why do you call her *your kitten?*" Gabriel asked in French.

"Because I like her claws." Raphael replied with a look at his brother that ended any further discussion on the subject.

Gabriel freed one hand and went to work on the opposite wrist. "What happened with Mathilde?"

Raphael flicked her a glance and narrowed his eyes as if assessing how much she understood.

A certain level of fluency was expected from educated women of her class.

Mercy found something fascinating on her own manacles, refusing to look up at him.

After a pregnant pause, he said. "We will discuss it later. Where do we meet Marco?"

"By the Loo."

Mercy searched her French vocabulary for the word loo and found nothing. Did they mean the washrooms? She wrinkled her nose. Did they say that for her benefit? To throw her off maybe? The toilets were not a very fitting location for high-brow clandestine intrigue to take place.

But then, who was she to tell criminals where to convene?

"We have to go, we're almost to the bridge." Gabriel freed his brother's other wrist.

"You go. I'll lock up." Raphael motioned for the padlock, which Gabriel tossed to him before sliding out the door just as smoothly and silently as he'd arrived.

The springs depressed just slightly when the cart was alleviated of his weight. The Goliath of a man stepped off the tall carriage with the same grace a dancer would stride away from a curb onto the cobbles.

The ceiling of the cart was too short for Raphael to stand, so he stooped toward her as he reached his long, muscled arms out to the side in the stretch of a free man.

"Here." Mercy lifted her wrists. "Release me!"

Instead of taking her manacles, he gathered the hands she offered into his large, rough palms, his thumb running over wrists made raw by her struggles.

And just like that, they were no longer in a cage. No longer was she shackled by iron...but instead a velvet rope wound its way around her limbs, cording and knotting her to him.

She felt at once vulnerable and invincible.

Safe and in peril.

The fresh, expensive scent of him overpowered the staler odors of the carriage. His eyes were mesmerizing, taking up the entirety of her vision, forcing everything else to fall away.

Forgotten.

He moved with such swiftness, and yet when his lips sealed to hers, the press of it was astonishing in its gentility. His neck corded with tension, his shoulders bunched, and his grip tightened.

But his mouth. Oh, his mouth. It sampled her with a series of light strokes, restraining his ardent passion with well-practiced skill.

Mercy forever displayed the wrong reactions to stimuli. This time was no different.

Any space in her temper for anger or aggression was overtaken by an abject exhilaration. An undeniable excitement that bordered on impatience.

Though it was increasingly cold, they built their own fire, igniting something between them that had a portent of inevitability.

An inarticulate sound vibrated from somewhere deep within him, quickening her heart and rushing the blood through her veins with an injection of heat.

She surged closer, her fingers gripping his collar as the kiss deepened of its own accord. She couldn't tell whose mouth opened first, but their tongues met and danced.

Sparred.

In this moment, they had their own language. One that was as lilting and lyrical as any that existed. It was guttural and tonal and it gathered responses from her she never thought herself capable of making.

She knew there was more. More of this wild storm building between them. More of this man she wanted to explore.

More of the world she wanted to see.

Wanted him to show her. To teach her.

Dangerous. A voice warned from somewhere far, far away. Someplace buried so deep in her psyche, she might have forgotten it even existed.

Her reason. Her wit.

He'd interred it beneath the avalanche of desire

tumbling through her, tossing her end over end until she couldn't decide which way was up.

Danger. You're in danger.

The warning was closer now, more urgent. Enough to draw her back, breaking the seal of their lips.

She only had a moment of gratification at a similar haze unfocusing his stormy eyes before the clouds parted and he blinked down at her with an expression both alert and regretful.

"Forgive me," he whispered, releasing the lock on her shackles and letting them fall to the floor.

She looked down at them in mute astonishment, not having even noticed he'd been working on them.

By the time she'd registered that he moved, he'd slid out the door and pulled it shut and secured the padlock just as she lunged for him.

"Wait!" she cried, wrapping her fingers around the bars. "You're going to let me rot in jail while you go free?"

Now that they were in a busier part of the city, she could hear the astonished gasps and exclamations of the passersby.

He hung from the carriage by one hand at the hinges of the door and one foot on the ledge as he grinned into the cart through the barred window.

"I know who your family is, Mercy Goode, you'll be back home in time for tea." His eyes were no longer glinting, but ablaze with silver light.

Rage surged inside of her, fueled by the heat still thrumming and throbbing through her.

"You know nothing about my family, you merciless cad," she hissed. "You're lucky I'm locked in here or I'd—"

"You'd do something reckless, no doubt, like follow me..." He said this with a confounding sort of fondness. "And that's too dangerous. Even for you."

Frustrated. *Furious.* Mercy shook the iron bars once again, then shoved her hand through them, attempting to claw at his eyes.

He leaned back just in time, the thick locks of his hair fluttering in the draft coming off the roof of the moving coach as he barked out a laugh.

God, he was handsome when he smiled. Especially when his lips were glossed and a bit swollen from kissing.

She could cheerfully murder him.

Swinging back, he brought his face close to the bars, his eyes drilling into hers with that dizzying change they made from mirth to sobriety. "If we see each other again, Mercy Goode..." he warned in a voice made of sex and honey.

"Be ready for me to taste the rest of you."

CHAPTER 3

$\mathcal{T}$he reasons the jailers took a wide-eyed second glance at Felicity Goode were threefold.

The first being that she was exceptionally lovely today in a lavender gown threaded with violet ribbons and a matching velvet pelisse. The latter, cinched too tightly at the waist, accentuated the dramatic indent of her figure, and created a lovely backdrop for her cascade of flaxen hair beneath her smart hat.

The second was that the stunning midnight-haired woman on Felicity's arm was the wife of their most revered and respected Chief Inspector, Sir Carlton Morley.

Prudence, their second eldest sister.

This would be the first time these men might have seen her lately about, as she'd been kept frightfully busy doting on her infant twins, Caroline and Charlotte.

She was still apple-cheeked from pregnancy, her glowing dark eyes happy, if half-lidded by the sort of exhaustion only known to new mothers. She'd wrapped herself in burgundy velvet to make up for the pallor of her complexion.

And third, Felicity was the unmistakable mirror of

Mercy, who stood facing her from the other side of the dingy iron bars. Their resemblance was uncanny.

Most twins had a hint of identifiable difference. A freckle here, a jutting tooth or a divergent shade of hair.

For Mercy, to look at Felicity was to look in a mirror. Even their parents had an impossible time telling them apart.

Which, in Mercy's opinion, spoke volumes about them as parents.

More out of blindness than concern, Felicity squinted into the cell where Mercy had been blessedly alone for the better part of two hours. Though she'd terrible vision, she was urged to not wear her spectacles in public, as they were considered unflattering. This time, however, Mercy knew she'd eschewed her spectacles for a different reason.

One that was Mercy's own fault.

"Imagine, if you will, my surprise when a constable came round the house to inform Mama and Papa that *I'd* been arrested," Felicity huffed.

"Please don't be cross with me," Mercy begged her twin, wincing with shame. "I knew that if I gave them your name, someone would be more likely to come fetch me. Everyone likes you better."

"That isn't at all true," Prudence protested, tossing her curls with a saucy snap of her lithe neck. "You are both our beloved treasures. Now wait here whilst I fetch Sgt. Treadwell to unlock this cell so I can take you home and murder you in private. You're bloody lucky my husband is in court today." With an impish smirk she swept away, the train falling in gathers from her bustle, swishing with her efficient strides over the well-worn wood.

"Thank you, darling!" Mercy called after her, wrapping her fingers around the cold iron bars. The sooner she had her freedom the better.

She hadn't taken a full breath in hours.

Felicity, eyes wide with rapt incredulity, laced her fingers over Mercy's until they knotted around the bars together in a complicated grip. "Are you all right?"

Mercy nodded, though her beloved sister's affection was nearly her undoing. "Are Mama and Papa furious?"

At that, Felicity brightened a bit. "Actually, I received a postcard today in lieu of their arrival. They've decided to extend their stay on the Riviera another month, perhaps two. Perhaps if we can whisk you out of here without a scandal, they'll never have to know."

"You couldn't have brought me happier news!" Mercy blustered in relief. The Baron and Baroness Cresthaven, their parents, were two of the most pious, pinched-faced fuddy-duddies to ever hold a title. Any time they spent away from the house was like a ray of sunshine on a frigid, grey day in late winter.

Like this one, for example.

"Did you *really* strike an inspector?" Felicity whispered, glancing around to see if anyone stood nearby.

"Martin Trout." Mercy spat the words as if they tasted of his namesake. "He told me Mathilde *deserved* what her husband did. I *barely* swatted him." Mercy rolled her eyes as righteous indignation tightened her rib cage. "And he repaid me tenfold."

Tilting her head to display her bruising cheek, she enjoyed Felicity's clucking and tutting over the wound, now that she didn't have any handsome, smirking men to keep her chin up for.

"I have a poultice of parsley, arnica, and comfrey that will rid you of the bruise in half the time it would take to heal on its own," her twin promised. "Titus even had me make some for him to disseminate to his patients. Wasn't that wonderful of him?"

KERRIGAN BYRNE

Mercy's forehead wrinkled at the breathlessness in her sister's voice when Dr. Titus Conleith's name was spoken. He'd been a coal boy in their household when they were small, then a stable hand, and a footman as he'd grown into a man.

Though he was a few years younger, he'd loved their eldest sister, Nora, with a singular passion since the day he'd met her.

And, Mercy suspected, Felicity had loved him with the strength of a little girl's hero worship.

Titus was handsome in that rough-hewn, somber kind of way. Studious, deferential and ruthlessly clever. He was a man of unflinching principle and a fathomless well of patience. The very picture of a gentleman with the shoulders of a war hero and a reputation of the most respected surgeon in Blighty.

But to Felicity, he was the boy who'd squirreled away books for her to read and didn't poke fun when she used to pronounce her R's as W's.

"I hardly want to believe Mathilde is dead." Felicity's features crumpled with sorrow.

Mercy answered with a nod, gripping her sister's fingers tighter.

It was Felicity who'd met Mathilde first. She volunteered at the hospital sometimes, reading to the infirmed and holding new babies. Helping Titus mix tinctures or taking stock of the pharmacy.

She was as much a liability at the hospital as she was an assistance, since she fainted dead away at the sight of blood. No one had the heart to suggest she go elsewhere, for fear it would make her feel unwanted.

Felicity had spent the crux of her life being told that, as the fourth and last daughter in a string of disappointing female births, she'd been the reason her mother could have no more children.

And there would be no heir.

32

However, when Gregoire Archambeau had fractured Mathilde's wrist, landing her in the hospital, it had been Felicity who had coaxed the woman into seeking help with the Lady's Aid Society where Mercy volunteered her time.

The twins had decided then and there that they were genius to split their attentions thusly. To be able to provide women and their children comprehensive help both medical, emotional, financial, and even offer protection and relocation if necessary.

Felicity put a white-gloved hand to her heart as if the news of Mathilde's death had pierced it. "Did she...did she do it herself? Or was it an accident brought on by too much drink and—and such?"

They both knew what *and such* stood for. The cocaine and opium Mathilde had become a slave to.

"She was *murdered*," Mercy revealed with a grave frown.

Felicity gasped. "It couldn't have been Gregoire; I watched him mount the gangplank to the ferry and he didn't disembark again. He'll be in France by now."

"I know." Mercy pursed her lips. Lips that still tasted of Raphael, even hours later. Lips she kept pressing her fingertips to, remembering the pressure of a startling —*searing* kiss.

No. She couldn't let that indiscretion derail her. She had a murder to solve. Even Detective Eddard Sharpe didn't allow the sultry Miss Georgina Crenshaw to distract him in the middle of a case.

"You...found Mathilde's dead body?" Felicity sniffed as if holding in a torrent of emotion. "Are you all right? Was there blood? Did she suffer?"

Mercy wanted to spare her sister the answers to her rapid-fire questions, but her twin always knew when she was lying. "No blood. But yes, her death was... a violent one. Someone throttled her, and broke her neck."

Felicity released her hand to slide her fingers to her own neck. "Do you think it was her lover? Did you ever find out who he was?"

"You'll never guess," Mercy said, admittedly gorging a bit on the drama of it all.

"Tell me."

"Raphael Sauvageau." The name tasted lush on her tongue.

Just as he had.

Her sister blanched as pale as startled milk.

Felicity was, no doubt, remembering the night at the docks when she'd stumbled into Gabriel Sauvageau's arms. The man had been wearing a wicked mask and brandished a long, sinister blade.

He'd not cut her. In fact, he'd not hurt her in the least.

But they couldn't be certain he *wouldn't* have, had the night gone differently.

"What's this about Raphael Sauvageau?" Pru asked, approaching with a knobby, bent officer whose age dictated that the largest responsibility he could handle was the keys.

"Found with the dead body, he was," the sergeant rasped, shaking his finger at the door as if the man in question stood there. "You're lucky he didn't slit your throat before he escaped the prison cart. Or worse." He eyed Mercy with a grandfatherly warning.

"He was *arrested* with you?" Pru gasped.

"And he *escaped*?" Felicity cried at the same time.

"In the wind, that one. Unlikely we'll ever catch him again." Sgt. Treadwell attempted to thread the key into the lock three times before the tremors in his liver-spotted hand would allow it.

Mercy waited until they'd thanked the officer, who released her with a stern word and told her that Trout had dropped all charges when he learned who her family was.

No doubt, the inspector didn't want to be the man who'd struck Chief Inspector Carlton Morley's sister-in-law.

The *she struck me first* argument didn't hold much water.

Once they'd bundled into the coach, Mercy regaled them with the horrors of the afternoon as quickly as she could, knowing that once she got home, she'd have to spend at least an hour in the bath to scrub the day away.

She told them about everything.

Everything...but the kiss.

Their eyes were both big and round as the full moon when she finished her tale, and no one spoke for a full half minute.

It was Felicity who broke the silence. "Do you think the Fauves supplied Mathilde with all the...medicines she took?"

"Who else?" Mercy surmised. "They're brigands and we know they've smuggled cocaine before. Let us not forget the inconsiderate bastards didn't spring me from the prison cart. They left me there!"

"Yes, their most heinous crime, indeed." Pru chuffed out a little laugh as she studied Mercy with a quick, level look. "Did he truly break Trout's nose?"

"Possibly his jaw...and a few fingers." Mercy wondered how a man's features could be both savage and eerily blank all at once as he methodically put Trout in his place. "Sauvageau threatened to break every bone below the man's elbow."

"Did he?" Pru's lips quirked in a faint smile. "It sounds to me like he fancies you."

"I agree." Felicity nodded.

"Fancies me?" Mercy huffed, sliding her palms against one another, wishing they'd not taken her gloves on such a cold day. "Over the corpse of his freshly murdered lover? I don't care if he is the handsomest rake in the empire, I'd not consider such a thing in this lifetime."

Felicity chewed on the inside of her cheek, her eyes looking at some distant spot outside the window. "So, his brother leapt onto the carriage, picked the padlock, and sprang him without the drivers knowing? That sounds rather...Well, it's a bit extraordinary, isn't it? Like something out of an adventure novel."

"Extraordinarily infuriating is what it was." Mercy swatted Felicity's knee. "Or did you forget the part where they *left me there*? It's not funny!"

"I'm not laughing," Pru said from behind her hand as her shoulders shook with mirth.

"It was rather inconsiderate of them," Felicity rushed to concede. "No doubt they left you because they knew you'd be safe in police custody, whereas they were likely off to do something diabolical and undoubtedly dangerous."

Mercy didn't tell them that he'd said as much.

"I imagine they didn't want you following them." Felicity brushed aside the curtain of the coach to check on their progress through the city.

"I wouldn't have had to follow them," Mercy said mulishly. "I know exactly where they will be."

"Where's that?" Felicity asked.

"The loo at the zoo."

"Pardon?"

"I heard them talking, and while my French isn't perfect—"

"Your French is atrocious," Prudence teased.

Mercy ignored her. "They said they were going to meet someone named Marco in front of the loo at the London Zoo."

"They're not to meet at the toilet." Felicity remained distracted until she realized she'd said something out loud and then snapped her lips shut.

Mercy lunged, seizing her shoulders and shaking them. "What? Felicity, what do you know?"

Her sister gulped. "What will you do if I tell you?"

"What Detective Sharpe would do. Obviously."

"That's what I was afraid you'd say."

Prudence cut in, resting a motherly hand on Mercy's arm. "This isn't a storybook caper, Mercy, these men are lethal. You should tell Morley where they'll be. He'll find out about them for you."

"I will," Mercy vowed. "Tell me what you know, and I'll tell you where they'll be."

Felicity gulped, squinting at her for a different reason than her blindness. This time, it was true suspicion. "In French, the word spelled l-o-u-p is pronounced *loo*."

"And?" Mercy pressed.

"It means wolf."

Mercy's heart sped. "There you have it. They'll be at the wolf exhibit at the zoo at three o'clock."

Prudence reached into her vest and pulled out a dainty watch. "It's half five. We've missed them."

For once in her life, Mercy kept her mouth shut.

She'd also kept her promise. She'd told them where Raphael Sauvageau could be found.

Just not exactly *when*.

CHAPTER 4

A WEEK LATER

It turned out to be a beautiful day to plan a war.

Raphael Sauvageau loitered by the den of wolves at the London Zoo, idly watching across the way as two delighted children were given rides on the back of a sardonic-looking camel.

The morning had been blustery and grey. Stinging rain blown sideways by errant gusts pelted citizens who were brave or foolish enough to venture out. After luncheon, the rain disappeared as if someone had turned off a spigot in the sky, and celestial pillars of light pierced the late February clouds with the shafts of spring.

By three o'clock, the brick and cobbles of London glittered with gemlike droplets of golden light, and the city came to life, people bustling back into the streets.

The animals kept by the Zoological Society of London were likewise pleased with the changing weather. Zebras frolicked in their pastures and a giraffe licked a treat from out of the hands of a passing boy, who promptly burst into tears.

Adjacent to the zoo, the London elite flooded Regent's Park, eager to bask in the rare warmth and to hunt for any hint of emerging buds on the winter-bare flora.

Raphael watched the skeletons of the trees with grim detachment.

Knowing he would not live long enough to see them blossom.

What would *she* look like in the spring, surrounded by blooms shamelessly baring their colors for her? The most vibrant lily couldn't compete with the shade of her lips once they'd been plumped and pinkened by his kiss. The bluebell would wither in contrast to the hue of her eyes.

She was unlike anything or anyone he'd ever before encountered.

Mercy.

Even her name was a phenomenon he'd never known.

A concept he didn't understand.

It surprised him how powerfully he longed to explore her. Desired her to show him Mercy. In any form.

Her delectable form.

Indulging in a faint sigh, Raphael turned to see Marco Villeneuve saunter toward him, adjusting the diamond-encrusted cufflinks on his shirtsleeves.

A tittering group of schoolgirls in beribboned hats passed by, accompanied by their chaperone, a middle-aged woman with a sour face and cheeks drawn down by years of disappointment.

The handsome Spaniard touched the rim of his hat, and the ladies giggled.

When Raphael did the same, they sighed.

When he winked, two of them stumbled.

"You are shameless, *hermano*," Marco drawled, drawing closer and clasping his hand in fond greeting. Were they in their own countries, they'd greet with a kiss on each cheek.

Raphael scoffed. "Shame is a futile emotion crafted to plague those fragile enough to care what others think of them."

"Indeed." Marco leaned his shoulder against the wrought iron gate of the wolf enclosure and flashed his cocksure grin. Though his suit was of the finest craftsmanship, his chocolate-colored hair hung longer than was proper beneath his hat. It lent his tall, rangy form an untamed element that added to the dangerous allure he weaponized against women.

Intelligent females saw through him before he was able to break their hearts.

The others, well...they went away more cynical and suspicious of handsome rogues.

Marco slid his whiskey-colored gaze to the wolf enclosure and studied the five creatures as they paced and panted, eyeing the men as if to invite them in rather than warn them away.

They were of a kind, these beasts.

Raphael hated to see them caged.

One wolf, a dark, scruffy fellow with a blaze of white on his wide chest, climbed the hill that had been artfully arranged with boulders and soil to appear as if made by the chaos of nature. As the beast approached a lounging grey wolf, he flattened his ears and made a feral sound, yellow eyes snapping with ferocity.

The grey wolf bolted upright, relinquished his position, and slunk away, head and tail low as he found a new spot to rest.

The alpha sat above all.

"Well, *Jefe*, everything has been arranged as you instructed." Marco extracted a box of matches and lit a cigarette with a long draw before releasing the smoke on a heavy exhale. "Lord Longueville will be attending the Midwinter Masque, and will be likely to bring his generals from the High Street Butchers. You, Gabriel, and I will be present, of course, though I wonder if we should invite a third party to witness our conversation with Longueville. Word will spread that the battle for control of supplying vice to the *ton* is about to commence."

"I do not disagree." Raphael was careful not to let his complicated emotions show on his countenance. He was stirring trouble.

The lethal kind.

"I thought this was *loco*—I still do—but it might actually be crazy enough to work." Marco puffed out a breath filled with smoke and wonder before he glanced up. Whatever he read in Raphael's expression caused him to amend. "I should know better than to doubt you, *Jefe*."

Raphael waved his hand, absolving him of all that. "We Fauves do not follow without question. We are predators, not sheep, and we must be cunning. Question everything."

"As you say." Marco's head dipped in deference.

The hierarchy of the Fauves was not unlike those of the wolves. Intricate, subtle, and yet, brutally uncomplicated. There were no figureheads. No pomp or ceremony. There was the uncontestable leader of the pack. The alpha and his subordinates.

He was the one who led the hunters to their prey. And he was the one who took first blood. He claimed the greatest bounty before the rest of the pack fell upon it like scavengers.

But as the leader, it was incumbent upon him to provide, to remain uncontested. Or, if he was challenged, he must meet it with all the dominant ferocity of any king of beasts.

He had to win. Every time. To prove he was fit to lead.

That he was a man to be followed.

The mantle threatened to smother him sometimes.

But what else could he do? What else did he know?

Nothing.

This was all he was. All he had. A legacy of vice and villainy and a lifetime of lies. He was a man whose past was nothing but shifting shadows and secrets, and his future was—

An endless wasteland coated with the same.

Battles and blood, until one day a lesser beast would challenge him...and tear his throat out.

He'd have to.

Raphael was not the sort of man to submit to the sovereignty of another.

"Are you second-guessing the plan?" Marco queried, peering up from beneath the lowered brim of the hat. "If this goes awry, there will be blood."

"There's always blood," he quipped. "This will be no different."

Blood. Both red and blue.

He was playing a dangerous game, pitting his enemies and allies against each other.

A game where there would be victors, but no one truly won.

"No second thoughts," he clarified. "All has been prepared except—"

A flash of light struck him blind for a moment and he winced, blinking rapidly. When he opened his eyes again, it was gone, leaving a disorienting shadow in his vision as if he'd glanced directly at the sun.

Once his vision cleared, he found the culprit immediately upon searching over Marco's shoulder.

The sun had reflected off binoculars peeking over a shoulder-high hedge.

No, not binoculars. A shiny gold pair of opera glasses.

Gold, like the lovely ringlets surrounding said item.

A charming coiffure held in place by butterfly combs and garnished with baby's breath.

Detective Eddard Sharpe would be proud of this intrepid investigator. He was often quoted in his books as saying that when a necessary implement was not readily at hand, a true investigator improvised.

Opera glasses of all things. Raphael couldn't fight the tremor of a smile softening the corners of his lips.

Christ, but Mercy Goode could not be more endearing.

She'd, no doubt, donned her taupe, high-necked coat in the hopes of blending with the crowd. However, the light color actually caused her to stand out amongst people swathed in grey or black wool jackets against what had once been intemperate weather.

Who wore beige to the zoo on a wet day?

Of course, she'd understood the conversation he and Gabriel had in her presence. Gentle ladies were taught French, weren't they?

Marco, realizing that Raphael's notice had been directed elsewhere, glanced behind him to find the culprit. "What is it?"

"Nothing," Raphael said, shifting his gaze to the side. "I saw someone I recognized."

"Not the police, I hope. They are searching for you in every nook and shadow of the city."

"Which is why I'm hiding in the sunlight."

Marco chuckled and tapped his temple. "Always a step ahead, *Jefe*. That's why you're in charge."

Raphael put a hand on Marco's solid shoulder, only half meaning the fond gesture as he drew the gangster toward the lion's den—in the opposite direction of the curious girl. "I'm avoiding a woman," he explained as he ducked them behind a shed and then quickly changed their direction.

"Say no more." Marco winked conspiratorially and kept up with nimble strides.

Raphael got to business as he led Marco toward a back gate. "I had you meet me here because Dorian Blackwell is said to be fond of taking his children to Regent's Park in the late afternoon. Sometimes they come to the zoo, sometimes not, but I need you to find him and invite him and his most trusted men to the masquerade."

Marco's eyes widened. "Dorian Blackwell? The Blackheart of Ben More? He and his men ruled this city not so long ago, but everyone says he's reformed since he married a Countess. Retired, even."

Raphael inclined his head. "I think he would be interested in a market share of this product. He still holds enviable economic influence, from the dregs of the underworld all the way to Parliament."

Marco's eyes flashed with greed. It was something Raphael knew he could always rely upon...a man's own self-interest.

"Consider it done." Marco crushed his cigarette beneath his bootheel and strode toward the zoo's gate, one hand on the lapel of his dandy plaid suit. He held said gate open to a fine elderly couple who thanked him with wide smiles.

They'd miss their valuables later.

Raphael doubled back toward the wolf exhibit.

Flattening his back against the reptile enclosure, he peered around the corner to find exactly what he thought he would.

Mercy Goode standing before the wolves, forehead wrinkled and plump lips tightened into a recalcitrant frown.

He'd lost her and she resented him for it.

Poor thing. He wanted to tell her it didn't detract from her considerable detective skills. He was a professional criminal, and she little more than an inquisitive girl.

She had no chance of capturing him.

It surprised him to find that his hand had found its way inside his suit coat, to rest over his chest.

She made the muscles around his lungs squeeze at the same time his heart seemed to double in size and radiate a confounding warmth.

Kissing her in the carriage had been a mistake.

And yet, when he searched what passed for his conscience, he couldn't find it in himself to regret it.

Since the first moment he'd laid eyes on her, he'd been transfixed.

Beguiled.

No one that bold and brash should have such innocent eyes.

She was a force of nature, like a firestorm or an earthquake. Something that left the terrain forever altered in her wake.

She was unforgettable. Indescribable. Delectable.

How could he go to war without tasting that for himself?

Especially when she'd looked at him in *that* way. With the heavy-lidded gaze of a woman who wanted to be kissed but was too proud to ask and too untried to take what she wanted.

Raphael bit into his fist. He couldn't tell which was a more exquisite hell. Wanting to taste her? Or having sampled her flavor, knowing that a more sublime pleasure awaited the man who unlocked the passion roiling beneath the barely contained surface of her propriety.

Knowing, without a doubt, that he could release her like a volcano, and watch as she erupted into ecstasy.

He should go. He had so much to do, to prepare for.

He needed to be rid of her. For both of their sakes.

Visibly deflated, Mercy stowed her opera glasses in

the velvet pouch hanging from her wrist and turned to contemplate the wolves.

They'd come alive at her approach, panting and pacing, some of them making wild, hungry sounds.

Raphael knew exactly how they felt.

His feet carried him toward her as if moving without his consent. There was no stopping this, he was propelled—*compelled*—by her mere presence. She was, indeed, like the sun, and he was merely a helpless body trapped in her orbit.

How could he leave when she appeared so glum? How could he be the cause of such a frown?

He'd done some terrible things, but her displeasure would bother him all day.

So intent was she upon her disappointment, she didn't mark his approach until he spoke. "I always pity them, the predators," he murmured as he drew abreast of her, standing close enough that their shoulders nearly touched.

Other than a lift of her bosom with a sharp intake of breath, she made no move to acknowledge him.

Raphael leaned against the iron bars of the enclosure, watching the alpha pace back and forth. Staring deep into eyes that seemed so ancient and feral, compared to this so-called civilized place.

His chest ached for them both. "I wonder what it would be like to be as they are. Creatures of instinct and insatiable hunger...caged but longing to roam free."

Mercy tilted her chin to level him a sharp look, scoffing gently. "I am a woman. I don't have to wonder such things. I already know."

A pensive sound escaped him on a huff of breath. "It has never been a mystery why men keep women caged by so many unseen confines," he said. "Their laws. Their clothing. Societal expectations...And through doing this, men have devised the most fiendish jailers."

"Yes, you men have fashioned yourselves as most cunning oppressors," she agreed with an arch bitterness in her voice. "Congratulations."

"No," he purred, turning toward her. Inching closer. "Women's greatest enemy is other women. If you ever stopped competing for the favor of your oppressors and rose up against us, instead, we men wouldn't stand a chance."

At this, she shifted, her sharp chin dipping so she could study him from beneath the veil of her lashes. "You speak as though you're an expert on the subject of my sex."

"Women are too complicated and varied for one man to become an expert," he said, rather modestly, he thought, congratulating himself.

Her eyes narrowed further, reminding him of a cat irked by the attentions of a tiresome human. "Is it women who are complicated? Or men who are just too simple or fatuous to figure out what should be painfully obvious?"

He held his hands up in a gesture of surrender. "You're right, of course. Let us not say complicated. Let us say...intricate. Comprised of so many parts both fragile and indestructible. Mechanisms of emotion and logic, trivialities and also infinite wisdom."

He motioned to the wolves. "We men are the beasts. Quarrelsome and querulous creatures of instinct and desire."

"Is that why you call your gang *the Fauves?* The wild beasts. Because you are encouraging such animalistic behavior?"

Raphael nodded, wondering why it sounded wrong when she said it, why it pricked him with defensiveness. "My father invented the name and our creed. We were beasts before we fashioned ourselves men, and built our own cages of law and order. But once, we had the morality of a wolf. The ferocity of a bear. Cunning and speed of a viper."

"A viper." She held up her finger as if to tap an idea out of the sky. "That is what you are."

He contemplated the word. "I've been called worse."

"Worse than a snake?"

He lifted a shoulder and loosened it again. "I don't mind snakes so much. They're clever creatures... They're only villainized because of the one who tempted Eve."

She swatted the air in front of her as if batting his words away. "I find that story patently ridiculous."

"Do you?"

She rolled her eyes and tossed her head like a skittish mare. "We haven't the time for me to count the ways."

"I'd still love to hear you do so," he murmured, finding that he wanted very much, indeed, to know what she thought about anything. Everything. He found her relentlessly entertaining. "Another time, perhaps."

"I'm not planning on spending an inordinate amount of time in your presence." Gathering her skirt, she shifted away from him as if she needed space.

Distance he didn't want to give.

"You're angry with me," he prodded.

"Have you forgotten that you escaped the law and *left* me to face it? What sort of nefarious reprobate does that?"

"I knew you'd done nothing wrong, and that your family would close ranks and protect you. In my defense, I had business only a nefarious reprobate could conduct. Since you are not one, I couldn't very well be responsible for your safety."

Her chin jutted at a stubborn angle. "I'm an investigator, not an idiot. I wouldn't do anything unduly perilous. Also," she glared at him as if she could bore through his middle with the blue fire in her eyes, "you kissed me, you impolite blackguard! Without my permission, I might add."

"Ah, for that I *would* ask your forgiveness, Miss Goode..." His mouth softened and curled up at the memory. "If you had not kissed me back."

"I *never*!" She pushed away from the wolf enclosure and stomped toward the gate, her skirts swishing angrily.

"I know what animal *you* are," he teased, ambling after her with his hands shoved in his pockets.

So he did not give in to the impulse to reach for her.

"I am no other creature than woman."

"You are a fox," he corrected. "Playful. Clever...cautious and elusive. Yes. You, Mercy Goode, are a vixen."

"What I *am* is growing tired of your company," she snapped.

"Might I remind you that you were the one who followed me here?"

She whirled on him, her little nostrils flaring and her eyes sparking with azure storms. "I—that—I mean —" She pressed her lips into a frustrated hyphen before gathering her response. "Don't you dare for one *minute* feel flattered. I was investigating you. To see if you were doing anything despicable. I didn't come for *you*, but to gather information that would help Mathilde."

Oh, that he could make her *come* for him.

Raphael drank her in. She was lovely when she was angry. Her Cupid's bow mouth pursed and white at the edges with strain, her snapping gaze electric with color, and her little fists balled with fury.

She was so young. Perhaps too young for his thirty years. She glowed with an inner incandescence that didn't belong to this grey country. He wanted to sweep her away to a villa along the cerulean coast of his homeland. To strip her bare while white gauzy curtains danced in the sea breeze. He would let the sun kiss every inch of her pale skin just before his lips trailed in its wake.

"I want you to leave justice for Mathilde to me," he said, curling the fingers in his pockets into fists, so he didn't give in to the urge to sweep her hair away from the curve of her neck. "I will avenge her."

It would be among the last things he did.

"Avenge her?" Her eyes narrowed and she took a step closer, her ire at him thrown over for a clue. "Are you saying you know who is responsible for her death?"

"I have an idea."

"Who then?" she demanded.

She would never drag it out of him. Would never be drawn into his world. She was everything good and light and worthy. She was a beacon, one that both attracted him and warned him away.

Raphael changed tactics, taking a threatening step toward her. "You've already done something perilous. You came here. To find me... Alone."

He should have expected anything other than a retreat from her. "As you can see, sir, we are *not* alone." She gestured to the throngs of people, some passersby paying them a bit of curious attention.

"*We* are not alone," he conceded, drawing her hand into his to brush a kiss against the knuckles of her gloves. "But if you are with me...you are in danger."

"From whom?" She glanced about them dramatically, as if searching for the danger of which he spoke.

Surely some primitive instinct within her had to realize how close he was to—

"I'm perfectly safe," she said in a tone more convincing than confident. As if she were trying to persuade herself. "My—my brother-in-law, Chief Inspector Carlton Morley, is nearby."

"No, he isn't," Raphael tutted, advancing on her with measured steps. Forcing her to retreat in small increments. "I know Morley, he's as decisive as he is honorable, which means he'd have me in chains before I could do this."

Raphael seized her by the elbow and swung her into a deeply shadowed alleyway between two enclosures, with all the deftness of a man twirling his partner in a waltz.

He ducked them into the alcove of a door and slanted his mouth over hers, desperate to taste her before she could take in enough breath to protest.

CHAPTER 5

*B*ut she didn't.

She didn't struggle or fight.

The first time he'd kissed her, he'd taken her by surprise. She'd been unerringly sweet and obviously untried.

And still she'd captivated and aroused him more than the most skilled of courtesans.

She was artless. Guileless. And in her presence, he was something he'd never been before.

Helpless.

She didn't remain still or soft in his arms. She didn't become rigid nor limp with fear nor anger.

She went wild.

Her fingers were claws in the lapels of his jacket. At the taut muscles of his back. Then suddenly scoring his scalp as she turned his impulsive seduction into a battlefield. Her lips pulled tight against her teeth. Her tongue went on the offensive, thrusting into his mouth and tangling with his.

God, he'd only meant to pilfer a sip of her. Sample her particular confection of flavor and savor it.

But *she* devoured *him*.

Raphael's blood pounded in a deafening roar,

screaming through his veins with a victorious thrill. His entire body was consumed with the taste of her, like a crisp, sparkling Alsatian summer wine, both tart and sweet, with a sultry bite.

She intoxicated him.

Her ferocity called to something inside of him.

Because he knew it for what it was. Both an attack and a defense. He'd cornered her, and so she would make certain she was in control by claiming the kiss.

And he didn't want that.

What he wanted was her to enjoy it.

Bracketing her face with his hands, Raphael brushed tender thumbs over the downy curve of her cheekbones as he fought back the savage lust that hardened his body. He longed to take her. To possess and invade her, to thrust into her with the same abandon she showed now.

Images tormented him. Of her bent over things, tied to other things, writhing at the wickedness he could wreak upon her.

It tantalized him to the brink of madness.

And yet.

Some foreign sort of affection welled within him. While his body was hard, inside his rib cage, something loosened.

Softened.

This was not a moment to conquer.

But to seduce.

He brushed his thumbs to where their lips met, and nudged at the corner of her mouth, drawing it open and slack. He broke the seal, unhooking their tongues. Instead, he dragged his slick lips over hers in languid, gliding motions. Once. And again. Coaxing her to respond.

She reacted just how he'd hoped, her arms more

embracing than clutching. Her hands kneading rather than clawing.

God, he could live to make this kitten purr.

Had there ever been a woman so perfectly rendered for kissing?

Her curves were more pronounced next to the hard planes of his own body, her breasts straining against his chest, her hips flaring dramatically when his hands charted the indent of her waist to rest there.

Somewhere in the distance, a lion roared. A child squealed.

The sounds broke her of whatever thrall he might have held.

Small hands flattened against his chest before she gave a mighty shove.

Raphael allowed it, retreating several steps.

Glowering in his direction, she wiped at her lips with the back her gloves, as if scrubbing the taste of him away. "You must stop doing that," she commanded. "It's—It's—"

"Delicious?" he supplied helpfully.

"Disgusting," she spat.

"You did not seem disgusted to me," he taunted. "What I think you are, is afraid."

"I am *not* afraid of you." She circled him like he might be a predator about to attack, inching toward the entrance to their intimate alley.

Raphael tried not to examine why he felt the small distance between them in the very essence of himself. The pads of his fingers, the fine hairs of his body. They seemed tuned to her by some magnetic force, drawing him forward.

"Are you afraid you'll like me?" he challenged. "That you'll want more?"

"N-no." Her eyes darted this way and that as she took two more steps backwards.

"Why are you retreating, then?"

She froze. Blinked. Then squared her shoulders, drawing herself up to her full—if less than impressive —height.

"I'm not retreating, I'm—I'm leaving. There's a difference." Spinning on her bootheel, she hurried until she reached the end of the alley, and flounced around the corner.

When Raphael caught up, she was strolling toward the entrance, quite obviously doing her level best to keep her footsteps steady so not to appear as though she fled.

He should let her go.

He should turn around and put her behind him. Focus on the task at hand and not give in to the strange and unmistakable lure.

It was as if she had his heart affixed to a spool of string like a kite, and he trailed after her—above her— in quivering anticipation of the moment she would pull him out of the wind.

No good could come of this. He...should...just...

"I'll squire you out." The offer slipped from his lips before he could pull it back.

She rewarded his chivalry with a sharp glare. "I hardly need a squire, and don't require your company."

"Evidently not, but in order to quit the zoo, I also need use of the gate."

"There's the other entrance." She pointed toward the back where he'd left Marco.

"Alas, this one is the one I prefer." He offered a gesture of regret that conveyed *there's nothing to be done*, and sauntered after her.

She made an exceedingly unladylike sound of exasperation and quickened her pace. "Just keep your hands and your lips to yourself."

Raphael lengthened his strides, having no issue

keeping up with her. He breathed in the frigid air tinged with her singular scent, and didn't even lament the clouds as they drifted toward the sun in a threatening manner.

Even at the bitter end of winter, when all tended to be grey and gloomy, she smelled of sweet herbs and sunshine, evoking memories of sipping pastis on sundrenched verandas of the Mediterranean.

The shadows could not touch her. The grey couldn't dim her, no matter how it might try.

And he was a moth mesmerized by her flame.

A vendor called to her, holding out paper wrapped around candied nuts.

"No, thank you," she said as she bustled on by.

He trotted to catch up. "You're a lady of taste, surely you can spare a coin for—"

Raphael maneuvered himself closer and it only took a censuring look to send the man scampering in the other direction.

"Unbelievable," she muttered beneath an irate breath.

"You're welcome." He flashed her a winsome smile as if he'd not caught the sarcasm in her voice, and clasped his hands behind his back to make himself seem more casual.

She whirled on him, thrusting a finger at his chest. "What is the matter with you? Do you enjoy throwing your strength and malice into the faces of those less powerful? Do you prefer it when people fear you? Does it lend you some perverted sort of thrill?"

"Of course not," he defended, running the tip of his tongue over lips that still tasted of her. "I get my perverted thrills elsewhere."

"Bah!" She threw her hands up in an ironically violent gesture of defeat and stomped away, abandoning all pretense of composure.

Thoroughly amused, Raphael fell into step with her. "I shouldn't like *you* to fear me," he explained.

"As I said, I do not, but you just intimidated that poor man back there."

"I didn't want him to hassle you."

"No, of course not, when you're doing such an excellent job of it."

He sighed, hating that he felt the need to explain himself to her as he had no one else in his entire lifetime. "Fear isn't something I find enticing, merely...useful."

"Useful?" She wrinkled her forehead in puzzlement as if she couldn't fathom how or why anyone would use such an awful, powerful phenomenon. "You mean, in your criminal enterprise?"

"Yes."

"You make men fear you so that you may control them." She said this with conviction, as if she had experience in the matter.

Keeping his hands distinctly clasped behind him— so as not to give in to the overpowering urge to once again pull her against his body—Raphael surprised himself by telling her the truth. "There is a difference between leading men and controlling them. Again, I *prefer* people not fear me."

"But you *just* said you use—"

"It does me no good to incite terror of *me*, per se," he clarified. "If I have an enemy, I find out what they already fear and turn it on them. I figure how to sow it among their own ranks until the right eye doesn't trust what the left eye sees. I can make it so the heart and the brain fear each other, and then the muscles and blood don't know whom to obey. When men fear what they used to love, that fear often turns to hate. And then they rip out their own hearts. They pluck out their own eyes... They devour themselves."

"That's..." To his abject astonishment, she was quiet for five entire steps before conjuring a word. "Diabolical."

"That, *mon chaton*, is when I strike. When they are blind. When they'll never see me coming."

"Oh." She looked off into the distance, melancholy sitting strangely on her face. As if it didn't belong. "I do not think Mathilde ever saw her killer coming. At least... I hope she did not. That she wasn't afraid."

Lanced by the selfsame ardent hope, Raphael asked, "Why did you come seek me out when I'm wanted for Mathilde's murder?"

"Because I...I don't think you killed her."

"You would not have kissed me back if you did."

"I did *not* kiss—"

He interrupted her protestation. "What makes you think I am innocent?"

"I don't have to tell you," she said, still stubbornly refusing to look at him.

"Please."

The soft word caused a hitch in her step. Perhaps she heard the desperation in it. The earnest grief he'd been keeping at bay.

Sighing, she relented. "For one, your shoes were impeccable and expensive, and the boot that left the mud on the window was grooved like that of a Brogan. A man's military boot, but this one was higher, like a woman's. I can make no sense of it."

"I could have changed shoes." He played the devil's advocate.

"Unlikely." She pursed her lips, chewing on the bottom one with a pensive frown. "Also, her neck was snapped in a motion that signified her murderer was left-handed, and I've noticed your right hand is your dominant one. And besides... I credit you with more intelligence than to stay at a crime scene long enough for the body to cool."

Raphael did his best not to preen. She was a woman who didn't give much credit. It was strange how much even a tiny compliment like that seemed to stir him.

"Who told you we were lovers?" he puzzled aloud. "Mathilde wasn't the type of woman who revealed her secrets, not with Gregoire as a husband."

At the question, she looked over at him, and the concern he read in her eyes almost caused him to stumble. "Don't be cross with her. She didn't use your name. Merely revealed to me that you were young, dark, dangerous, powerful, and that you were—"

She broke off, her gaze skittering away.

The color darkening her cheeks, still flushed from his kiss, intrigued him. "I was, what?"

"It doesn't matter. It has nothing to do with the case."

"I'd still like to know. If it was something Mathilde thought of me."

At that, she conceded. "She intimated that you were...rather skilled."

He snorted his disbelief. "Mathilde didn't use such banal terms as 'rather skilled.'"

"All right," she hissed. "She told me you were capable of passion she'd never known a man to possess. That you knew a woman's body as if you'd created it for your own skill. She said that no lover had ever made her perform such wicked acts. Had never made her want to."

Raphael flashed her his most charming smile. "Well, Mathilde was many things, but she wasn't a liar."

"No. She wasn't." For once, there was something they agreed upon. "You revealed yourself by being there the moment her husband traveled away."

"So I did," he said, just realizing it, himself.

"Did you love her?"

She seemed as surprised to ask the question as he was to hear it, and he had to cast about his heart for an answer.

For the truth.

"I was...fond of Mathilde. But there is only one person alive that I can profess to love."

"Yourself?"

Her clipped answer surprised a bark of laughter out of him. "You know me better than you ought to for only having met me twice before."

"A detective is trained to make keen observations about people." She tapped the spot beneath her eye with her fingertip, indulging in a satisfied smile.

"A shame none of the detectives they sent after me were women."

"You'd be caught by now, no doubt."

"I imagine you are right."

She lifted her hand to her eyes, shading them from the quickly dissipating sun. "I've observed something else."

"What is that?"

"We are being followed."

CHAPTER 6

*M*ercy suddenly wanted Raphael Sauvageau to live up to his name.

He was just so unnervingly cool and infuriatingly collected. All loose limbs and unaffected insouciance, even as he checked their periphery for a threat.

As if finding one wouldn't at all ruin his day.

If this man had as much sway over fear as he claimed, then what was it that could send him into histrionics?

Everyone feared something.

You terrify me, Mercy Goode.

Surely, he'd been joking.

He gave their surroundings a surreptitious examination. "Does the man following us have a billycock hat and a grey morning suit with the paper tucked under his left arm?" His lips barely moved as he peered off into the opposite direction of the man in question.

A lance of trepidation speared her gut. "You've spotted him, too?"

Turning, he lifted his hand in a wave at their voyeur.

Mercy almost slapped it out of the air before he informed her, "His name is Clayton Honeycutt. He's one of my Fauves."

"You're being followed by your own men?" she asked in disbelief, blinking over at their shadow, who nodded in greeting.

"We tend to trail each other. To go very few places alone. Our backs are never exposed, and it keeps us honest—well—at least among our own."

Something about the way he said this caused her to examine him more closely. He was being wry...and yet...a tightness appeared at the corner of his mouth that hadn't been there before.

"You have a good eye," he praised. "An admirable instinct for such things. Not many people can pick us out of a crowd like this."

Mercy tried to hide that his words pleased her, and found it impossible.

So delighted was she, in fact, that she neglected her defenses against him for a rare, vulnerable moment. Forgot that his masculinity was honed to a razor's edge, wielded with masterful ease. That his musculature was well-thewed and sculpted like that of a lean predator, one that relied on his speed and stamina as well as his strength.

One that moved about the world with nothing to fear.

And everything to claim as his own.

It became increasingly hard to believe that such a charismatic man, radiating a sort of godlike beauty, walked among mortals like her.

She forgot that she'd promised not to be charmed by him. Not even intrigued.

Let alone enthralled.

Her moment of weakness was all he needed.

His glittering grey gaze, like the silver tip of an arrow, found a chink in her armor and skewered her right through.

He looked at her as no man ever had. As if his eyes

only ever sought after her. As if they only knew her, and no one else. No other woman.

And that was a dangerous lie.

One he hadn't exactly told her, and yet she found herself wanting to believe it.

She needed to quit his company, before she let something more dangerous than a kiss happen...

Before she initiated it.

Marching forward, she kept her eyes on the gate, needing to think of something—anything—other than the kiss he stole from her.

The tender sweep of his lips across hers.

"I don't think Mathilde loved you either," she said, half to consider the notion, and half to whip him with it.

"Pardon?" His voice held an edge she didn't want to look over and identify just now.

"Well, when she wanted to escape her brutal husband, she came to the Lady's Aid Society...rather than to you. Why do you think that is, Mr. Sauvageau?"

"I couldn't rightly say..." He sounded pensive. Troubled. And Mercy was glad to hear it, because it made this man seem human.

"Did she tell you she was leaving?" Mercy ventured. "Did she ask you to go with her?"

He was silent for a beat longer than she expected an honest man to be. "No. I knew Gregoire was going back to France, but I was not privy to Mathilde's plans to leave him, even though I'd demanded she do so many times."

"Would you have gone with her if she asked?" Mercy slowed her march. Suddenly the gate was getting too close, and she didn't feel as though she could breathe until she heard his answer.

Which was patently absurd.

"No," he said again, his tone measured with a

chemist's precision. "Mathilde knew me too well to ask."

She could think of nothing in reply to that, so she drifted silently forward for a while. Usually, the beavers and waterfowl in the gardens would charm and distract her, but today her notice was captured by a different sort of beast.

It was he who broke the silence. "Mathilde had a ball to attend the night after next, she'd have considered it the greatest tragedy to miss it."

"Indeed." Mathilde had informed Mercy of the Midwinter Masquerade being held at Madame Duvernay's. All of the *demimonde* would attend. Famous actresses and courtesans. Women who were kept by dukes and royalty. Mediums and occultists, writers and scholars, indeed, artists of all renown and modality.

These had been her people, and Mathilde had wanted to say goodbye before she left forever. She was most adamant about it, in fact, making furtive explanations about people who she might see.

Might her murderer have tried to stop her from attending?

"What will you do now, Miss Goode?"

His question broke her reverie. "Nothing's changed. I intend to find Mathilde's murderer, of course. Don't think I've forgotten that you mentioned you might have an idea of who it could be."

His eyes shifted, as if sifting through the truths to give her.

"There's no need for you to find a lie," she prompted. "You can tell me what you know. You can *trust* me."

His assessment of her was slow, but not languorous nor seductive as it had once been. This time, it was full of questions she couldn't define, and a cynical sort of sadness that slid through her ribs to tug at her heart.

"A man achieves what I have by trusting only that other people will betray him. In my world, naïveté is the chief cause of untimely death."

"How awful that must be." She grimaced with distaste. "Why anyone would join a world like that is beyond me."

"Some of us have no choice," he murmured, his eyes fixing to a far-off point. "Indeed, it is the belief of the Fauves that the entire world is just such a savage place. We merely chose to accept the fact, and then grant ourselves the greatest chance of survival in this jungle man has crafted for us."

Mercy considered this. Considered *him*. For the first time, she imagined that she peeled back the years from his sardonic beauty. Erased the cynical set to his mouth and the ever-present tension in his shoulders. She relieved him of the mantle of menace and the threat of violence, to uncover who he might have been once upon a time.

A boy. Carefree and mischievous. Precocious and witty with that disarming dimple in his left cheek.

What sort of variables formulated by the Fates created this man who stood before her?

What choices had he made?

What choices were made for him?

"How do you know, then, if anyone is ever giving you correct information?" she wondered aloud.

He pondered this. "Oftentimes, if they owe me, or if our interests align, that can make an ally for a time."

"Well, there we are then!" she exclaimed, clapping her hands together once. "I suppose I owe you for the gold you gave Nora and Titus, so—"

He shook his head in denial, and the sun shone blue off his ebony hair. "That was a payment for services about to be rendered. And I forfeited that to your sister and her husband, not to you."

"What about a transaction, then," she offered. "Surely that's a language you understand."

At that, his eyes flared with interest. "I'm listening."

"You tell me what I want to know, and then I'll tell you what information I have. A fair trade, wouldn't you say?"

His expression flattened. "Not the transaction I was hoping for, but... I suppose it'll do."

"Excellent." She offered her hand for a shake to seal their deal.

He took it, looking a bit bemused.

Even through her glove, she was suffused with the potency of his touch. Something as innocuous as a handshake with this man felt wicked.

Not wrong, per se.

Illicit.

She was aware of every tactile sensation. Of the rasp the very whorls his finger pads made on the silk. Of the restrained strength in his grip. The way he lingered over the gesture, as reticent as she to let go.

Clearing her throat, Mercy plucked her hand away and reached into her reticule, pulling out a notepad. "You first. Who do you suspect wanted Mathilde dead?"

Raphael's voice altered as he spoke, too heavy and low to be easily heard over the squeals of happy children, the sounds of unhappy animals, and the chatter of the London elite. "Mathilde was a woman of glorious highs and devastating lows. She often indulged in...substances to help her manage these riotous moods of hers. I knew this could be destructive, but I could not bring myself to admonish her for seeking to control her suffering."

"Did you provide her with these substances?" Mercy asked, careful to keep the judgment from her voice.

"Sometimes." He looked out over the heads of the crowd, as if searching the past. "She had spells when she seemed as though her energy would never cease. She did reckless, devastating things. Initiated brawls in public. Seduced other women's husbands. She even stole from me once to sell to her friends in the *demi-monde*. I'll admit I have killed for that, but I would never hurt a woman, least of all, her."

He couldn't even trust his own lover. The thought made Mercy desperately melancholy, even as he continued.

"After these spells, she'd sleep for an entire week, as if her very soul was weary." He blew out a sigh, as if fighting a bit of that weariness himself. "She and Gregoire relocated here from France to escape a scandal there," he continued. "Though she refused to give me details, I gathered that she was wanted for a theft from the Duchesse de la Cour. I have often wondered if she sought me out because she thought I could protect her. From her enemies...from herself."

He paused, and she thought she saw a very human emotion soften his chiseled features.

Regret.

"The Duchesse is visiting a cousin here in London, which causes me to wonder if she's reaped her revenge on Mathilde." His somber eyes found hers. "That is the lead I intend to follow."

Mercy tapped her pencil against the pad, biting at her cheek in thought. "Mathilde did say she had to conduct some final business before she left...do you think the Duchesse will be at this masquerade you mentioned?"

"I cannot say. I intend to find out before then." He rubbed a hand over his jaw, which seemed to be less smooth as the afternoon wore on. "It is your turn to relinquish information."

"What would you like to know?"

"What was the destination of her escape?"

That was an easy question to answer. "We were taking a train to the coast, and from there she was going to disembark to America."

Raphael nodded, a bleak smile haunting his lips. "She often spoke of seeing the Brooklyn Bridge. Of taking a train all the way to the Pacific Ocean." His face hardened and he turned to her. "You will not go after this murderer."

She bristled. "You cannot issue me orders as if—"

He sliced a hand through the air to cut off her protestations. "Has it occurred to you, Miss Goode, that this killer might think nothing of slaughtering *you* and degrading your pretty corpse before leaving it in the gutter, should you get in his way?"

"Of course it has," she sniped, doing her best to seem undeterred by his graphic warning. "I'm not planning on getting in his way, only finding him out. Then I'll turn the evidence over to the authorities. That is what an intrepid investigator does."

He shook his head the entire time she spoke, all semblance of charm and charisma replaced by a solemn determination.

"It's too dangerous," he insisted, leaning on every syllable for undue emphasis. "Leave it alone, Miss Goode. Leave it to me. You go back to your balls, your books, your seamstresses and your suitors. Live a long and privileged life for those of us who—"

"Ha!" She poked him in the chest and then shook her hand when her finger crumpled against steely muscle. "I'll thank you to note that I have no suitors at present, nor do I desire one, and I'd rather attend the dentist than a ball. So, do not presume you have the measure of me, sir."

He regarded her with resolute skepticism. "You mean for me to believe you don't love dressing in silks and having rich men trip all over themselves to offer for you?" He rolled his eyes. "Do go on, Miss Goode."

"I've plenty of interest and no offers." She crossed her arms over her chest, daring him to laugh.

Instead, he gave a dry snort. "Next you'll be telling me about blizzards in the Sahara."

"Don't be cruel," she admonished him. "It's patently obvious why no man would want me."

His smirk disappeared when he looked at her, replaced by a start of disbelief. "You're being serious."

"Deadly."

"I rarely find myself at the disadvantage of not knowing what someone in the *ton* finds patently obvious, as you put it... but I can't bring myself to imagine to what you are referring. I should think you have to beat the suitors away with a club."

Mercy squelched a threatening glow of pleasure at his words. His discombobulation seemed genuine, but he was a notorious charmer.

She refused to fall for it.

"It's not one thing," she explained, suddenly feeling itchy and defensive. Irate that she had to spell it out for him. "It's everything. It's *me*. I'm incapable of feeding the ego of a man with the insincere laughter or empty compliments they seem to require. I do not easily suffer fools, which means I have not ingratiated myself to many other debutantes or mothers of single noblemen. I read too much. I talk too much, which subsequently reveals that I am possessed of too many opinions." She began to count the reasons on the fingers of her hand. "I am political. Willful. Argumentative. Self-indulgent. All the things men abhor in a woman."

"Weak men," he murmured, a spark igniting in his gaze. "Perhaps you need someone other than the dandies of your class to tame you."

"Tame me?" His wicked suggestion aroused her, which irritated her in the extreme. "Don't make me laugh. I cannot abide the whims of any man, be he dandy or dominant. I do not desire to keep a household. I do not want to be known as Lady So-and-so, this man's wife. I want to be me. My *own* person." She paused in her passionate speech, amending it without hesitation. "Except for Felicity, of course. I couldn't live a life apart from her. We shared a womb. She's the other half of me. She possesses all the fragility and gentility I do not...and she suffers—"

Suddenly she froze. Realizing she'd revealed more to this man than any other. That she'd been on a tirade that must have dried up any interest he might have had.

And why should that matter?

"Suffers what?" he asked.

"Nothing. You needn't worry about her."

"Tell me," he prodded, and when she looked up into his arrested expression, she could believe that he really wanted to know.

That she hadn't frightened him away.

"Felicity...she has these conniptions. Spells, you might call them."

"Like Mathilde?" he queried.

She shook her head. "No. She is easily startled. Constantly trepidatious and worried. She has a hard time breathing, but not in the way of asthmatics. Her heart races and she will sometimes be sick or faint. She does faint an alarming amount. It's as if she stole all my fear for herself so I could be as I am. Brash and bold. We are a mirror of each other. And her reflection is so fragile. So gentle..." Mercy blinked at a stinging in her eyes. "Well, anyway, I would never leave her alone, and a husband would invariably ask me to. He wouldn't want for competition of my affections."

She looked up to find Raphael regarding her with

infinite tenderness. His eyes were not opaque or full of secrets. They were open. Challenging.

Burning.

No. He was not mysterious, this man. He wore his darkness. Advertised his sins. Pinned his emotions to his suit like a badge of honor.

"I don't want to go without ravishing you at least once."

Comprehension of his words didn't quite land at first. "Go where? Wait... What?"

He stepped closer, his expression intent. "I desire you like I have no other woman. I would take as many nights as you would offer, but I'll settle for just one."

Mercy blinked at him, certain she misunderstood his meaning. He was casual but serious. Relaxed, but intense. Surely, he wasn't asking if she would—

"Would you let me fuck you, Mercy Goode?"

Her mouth went slack, and she lost whatever substance held her bones together. She wished for a chair, a couch, a bench. Anything upon which to sink.

She looked around at the people. The families. This place that was so bustling and wholesome. Where propositions like his simply didn't belong.

Oh my. Mercy wanted to check her burning face for fever, but she didn't dare.

What was she right now? Upset? Insulted?

Enticed?

His eyes were searingly tender as he searched her face for an answer. "You are not slapping me. Or screaming at me. So, am I to imagine you are considering it?"

"You—were Mathilde's lover." And she was only deceased for a day's time.

At that, his features became impossibly kinder, his gaze containing admiration. "I have touched no other

71

woman since the night I gifted your sister with my gold."

"But that was...months ago," she marveled, doing her best to remember that she could not believe a word from his mouth.

He shrugged. "So it was."

"Mathilde made it seem as though she'd been with you not so long ago."

His eyebrows lifted. "Did she say that? That she and I had been lovers *recently?*"

"Come to think of it... no." She examined her reaction to that.

Her heart felt one thing.

Her body another.

His muscles remained lax, even though he allowed her to witness the uncontested hope radiating from him. "I assure you, Miss Goode, Mathilde and I did not share an understanding of any kind. Not in *that* way. There was nothing like romance between us, do you understand? I am doing her memory no disservice by propositioning you. I will be working harder to find her killer than the police. She will be avenged; you have my word. But I will be too distracted by my obsession with your lips to be of much use, unless you yield to me."

Swallowing around a sandpaper tongue, Mercy could only blink up at him.

For once in her life, she had nothing to say.

Because she was captured in the culmination of her eternal struggle.

The one between what she *should* do.

And what she wanted to do.

She might die an old maid, but she certainly didn't plan on being a virgin.

Suddenly, everything Mathilde told her about him

spun through her mind, sped through her blood, and landed in her loins.

The rapture he was capable of imparting. The pleasure. The desire. The stamina.

The sin.

He stepped closer, watching the war play out on her face, and spoke to tip the scales in his favor. "If you are to never take a husband, at least let me give you the knowledge of what to expect from a lover. Though I pity the man who next attempts to follow me."

The sheer arrogance in his claim should have turned her off of him instantly.

And yet, he said this with an odd sort of darkness. Like he pitied her next lover because he was already considering doing him violence.

"Let me have you tonight." His whisper sizzled through her.

"T-tonight?" she gasped out.

He made a gesture both helpless and sanguine. "I am a man for whom tomorrow is never a certainty, and so I live every night as if it were my last."

"How wondrous and terrible to not worry for tomorrow," she murmured.

"Wonderous and terrible. That is my existence in two words."

One of the wolves howled in the distance, a wild, mournful sound so foreign in the city.

Mercy turned toward it, needing not to look at him for a moment.

To catch her breath.

Was she truly considering this madness?

His breath was a warm caress against her ear as the clean masculine scent of him enveloped her. "Tonight, *mon chaton*," he purred from behind her, his finger skimming her shoulder blades so lightly. "Let me stroke you until you are exhausted with pleasure. Demand

73

what you want from me, I do not mind. Let me teach you what you deserve to know. What you should always expect. What your body is capable of."

Yes.

Mercy couldn't say the word, so she nodded.

She felt rather than saw him smile, even as he stepped back, granting her some space so she could finally breathe.

Pressing her fingers to her lips, she couldn't stop thinking about his tongue. Inside her mouth, it'd been warm and slick and tasted like depravity.

She'd been surprised it wasn't forked, devil that he was.

How would it be on other parts of her?

All her life, she'd hated the story of the serpent in the Garden of Eden. The allegory for temptation in the face of consequences.

She'd never understood why Eve bit into the apple.

Not until this very moment.

Not until this man with shining hazel eyes and a voice made of velvet and vice, tempted her beyond reason.

Trying to string her thoughts together, she stammered, "How would we...? Where will we? I mean..."

Her questions never found him she realized, as she turned back to clarify.

He'd disappeared.

CHAPTER 7

*M*ercy had often thought that for such a fair-complected man, Chief Inspector Carlton Morley was a bit of a dark horse.

Even as he paced the plush Persian carpets of her parents' solarium, his every movement was measured and controlled.

Carefully contained.

He was more compelling than handsome, she thought. His brow stern and the set of his jaw arrogant.

No, authoritarian. That was it.

A man who expected to be obeyed without question, likely because he was in charge of the entire London Metropolitan Police.

Which was why his choice of wife was so confounding. Her elder sister Prudence was ironically impetuous. But, Mercy supposed, her habitual *imprudence* accompanied a beauty of demeanor only matched by that of her soul, so it was impossible not to love her.

At least, in Morley's case.

They were ridiculously—disgustingly—happy.

For her part, Mercy couldn't begin to imagine being in love with a fellow who rarely relaxed and was always right.

And not in the way that most men *assumed* they were always right based on little more than their hubris and trumped-up opinions.

Morley was unfailingly well-informed and infuriatingly correct, more often than not. When he spoke, people leaned in to mark him because he was possessed of both power and practicality.

And that, Mercy was given to understand, was a rare combination of virtues.

Objectively, she supposed she understood why Prudence found him attractive, what with his corona of elegantly styled pale hair and eyes so cold and blue they might have been chipped from a glacier.

They only melted for Pru and the twins, becoming liquid and warm.

Mercy liked to watch the transformation her sister brought about in him, how his wide shoulders peeled away from his ears and every part of him seemed to exhale.

With his family, he could be charming. Cavalier, even.

He was protective and useful, honorable to a fault, and Mercy knew that beneath the furrow of disapproval on his brow was a wrinkle of worry for her. He watched them with the passionate overprotectiveness belonging to a man who'd once lost his own sister to tragedy.

It was why Mercy would suffer his warnings and lectures.

Because she knew that behind the bluster was a brother.

One who cared.

The Goode sisters were unused to compassionate men in their lives, having a staunch, religious father who maintained two demeanors where his family was concerned.

Critical or indifferent.

His greatest disappointment was not having a son, and he used his daughters like pawns in medieval land disputes, leveraging their reputations, fortunes, and beauty to garner him more prestige and power.

It entertained Mercy to an endless degree how often he'd been thwarted.

First by Pru, whose fiancé, the Earl of Sutherland, had been murdered moments before they were to walk down the aisle. She'd been arrested for the deed by Morley himself, and then rescued from the hangman's rope by a hasty marriage to the selfsame Chief Inspector.

Honoria—Nora—had done everything she'd been expected to, including marrying Lord William Mosby, Viscount Woodhaven.

That man was the most disastrous thing to happen to the Goode family. He abused Nora terribly, squandered all their money, and used their father's shipping company to smuggle illegal goods for none other than the Sauvageau brothers and their Fauves. Ultimately, he stole a crate of gold from the Sauvageaus and made dangerous enemies of them. His escape was foiled when he'd taken Pru hostage and Morley put a bullet through his temple.

My, but last year had been eventful.

Mercy wished for her sister now, wondering how much longer it would take for Pru to return from feeding Charlotte and Caroline.

Morley was like a pendulum of paternal disapproval moving back and forth in front of her as he lectured her about...well, about something or other.

The sermon had begun on the subject of her poking around murder scenes where she didn't belong, but she'd lost him some ten minutes back when he'd moved on to her arrest.

Here's why you shouldn't slap detectives and all that such nonsense.

She was generally inclined to answer back, at least to defend herself, but he'd already mentioned that Detective Trout had been dismissed for his heavy-handed retaliation against her.

Or would be, after he was released from the hospital due to the beating Raphael had inflicted. Now Morley was down one detective—albeit a mediocre one—during a crime wave.

That's where he'd lost Mercy's attention.

Her mind drifted from how "the entire situation could have been avoided if she'd not ventured where she ought not to have been in the first place." Et cetera and so forth.

No, drifted was the wrong word, it evoked the idea of aimlessness.

Her thoughts only ever went in one direction these days.

They were steered, propelled.

Captivated.

Would you let me fuck you, Mercy Goode?

The wicked proposition was a constant, obsessive echo in her mind.

It thrummed through her in Raphael's velvet voice, snaking its way into her veins and coiling deep in her loins.

Those words from any other man would have repelled her. She was someone who demanded deference. Someone who expected to be treated with the respect due her station. Not only as a gentleman's daughter, but as a woman—nay—a human being.

But, somehow, Raphael Sauvageau managed to make the profane query sound like a prayer.

A plea.

It was as though he'd asked, *Would you let me worship you?*

Because of the veneration in his eyes. The reverence that impossibly lived alongside the depravity in his gaze.

The pleasure in his promise.

He hadn't asked, *Would you fuck me?* The unspoken question being, would you pleasure me? Would you slake *my* hunger and fulfill *my* desires?

No. He'd offered to stroke her. To pleasure her. To teach her what to expect from a lover.

As if he would relish in providing her delight.

Mercy knew enough about lust to have felt the evidence of his desire against her skirts in the alcove where they'd kissed.

He'd been hard. He could have taken her right there.

His singular paradox of wildness and restraint called forth her own undeniable passions.

She'd not relented to his proposition because he'd wanted her.

But because she'd desired to take what he offered.

He was no sort of man to be allowed within miles of her heart, but her body?

His body?

Now there was a hard, rugged terrain she yearned to explore.

Mercy had to duck her head lest Morley read the wicked turn of her thoughts. She could feel her excitement burning hot in her cheeks, the tips of her ears, and...lower. Deep within.

Tonight.

She fought a spurt of panic. She still didn't know when. Or where. Or how. Or... when.

Would he dare come to Cresthaven? Would he send a message for a clandestine rendezvous somewhere?

What if he didn't?

She gasped in a breath. What if he changed his mind and didn't contact her at all?

What if she waited for him like a breathless ninny and he went off to some other strumpet, laughing at the thought of her pathetic virginal eagerness?

He was a degenerate, after all. A professional swindler.

She couldn't have imagined the intensity of his need, could she? Surely, she'd have seen through any sort of artifice on his part.

Unless he was a better deceiver than she was an observer.

Perish that thought.

The sound of Raphael's name, a foul word on Morley's tongue, brought her surging toward the surface from the murky depths of her ponderings.

"Who? What?"

Morley's brows, a shade darker than his hair, pulled low over his deep-set eyes. "Have you been listening to me?"

"Yes?" Mercy's eyes moved this way and that as she searched her empty memory for evidence against her lie. What had he just said?

He frowned with his entire face. "Is that a question?"

"No?"

"*Mercy*."

"You were...disparaging the leader of the Fauves, yes?"

He rolled his eyes and lifted his hands in a gesture of resignation. "I said, I do not like that you were alone with Raphael Sauvageau."

At that, she straightened in her seat, her spine suddenly crafted from a steel rod.

"Alone?" she parroted, her voice two octaves higher than usual. "Where did you ever hear such a thing?

Utter lies. There were people everywhere. We were *not* alone."

Except for when he'd kissed her.

Had someone spied their moment in the alcove?

"In the police carriage, Mercy, do try to keep up."

"Ohhh." She relaxed back with a relieved little laugh that ended on a sigh. "Well, yes, there was that time."

"To think you were locked up with him, right after he'd done Trout such violence..." His electric eyes bored into hers. "After he mercilessly executed Mathilde Archambeau. I promise you, Mercy, heads will roll for this. You should not have been subject to his company. You're lucky he didn't do you harm in his escape."

"You don't need to worry about that." Mercy waved away his concern. "Mr. Sauvageau didn't kill Mathilde."

With an aggrieved sigh, Morley sunk to her mother's hideous pink velvet chair, and leaned forward, resting his elbows on his knees and letting his hands hang between them. "And just how did the blighter manage to convince you of that?"

"He didn't," she informed him archly. "I deduced it."

"Deduced?"

"Yes. Deduced. A verb. It means to arrive at a logical conclusion by—"

"I know what it bloody means, Mercy, I'm simply trying to imagine how you could possibly have inferred evidence that my investigators had not."

Doing her best to keep her animation to a minimum, Mercy informed him about the open window, the boot print, the angle of poor Mathilde's neck and Raphael's right-handedness. She even drew diagrams, which—to Morley's credit—he studied very carefully before he looked up to regard her with new appreciation.

"I'm going to have to consult the coroner's report,

but if all is as you say, I think Raphael Sauvageau owes you a debt of gratitude."

Nothing could have dimmed the brilliance of Mercy's smile. Not only because her investigative skills had assisted in exonerating an innocent man—well, perhaps *innocent* was not an apropos word to use in reference to Raphael-Sauvageau—but also because she'd have the pleasure of informing said gangster later that night.

Probably.

If he showed up.

"I'm given to understand that Mathilde had an enemy in the Duchesse de la Cour over a theft back in France," she continued, holding up a finger as if to tap an idea out of the sky. "Perhaps the Duchesse and Mathilde's dastardly husband, Gregoire, were in cahoots."

"Cahoots," Morley chuckled.

"What?"

"No one uses that word."

"I use that word." Detective Eddard Sharpe used that word.

"You'd have made an excellent detective," he said with gentle fondness.

"Thank you." She primly smoothed her skirts over her thighs and rested her gloved hands on her knees. I was high time someone recognized that.

Someone other than Raphael, that is. He'd been the first to compliment her on her sleuthing skills.

Sucking in a deep breath, Morley heaved himself to his feet with the vital exhaustion of a new father and the responsibility of the entire city's safety on his shoulders. "We'll look into it."

"When?" she inquired.

"When we're able." He ran a palm down his face and glanced at the door through which his wife had disappeared a quarter hour past. "I should go find Pru."

"When will you tell me what you find?" Mercy stood as well, thinking she needed to bathe before tonight. "The coroner will have his autopsy done tomorrow maybe, the day after next?"

"I report to you now, do I?" Morley regarded her with a sardonic glare.

"I promised Mathilde I'd find her murderer."

His arch look softened. "And that is lovely of you, Mercy, but women like Mathilde—who keep the company she kept, and indulge in the vices she enjoyed— they often find themselves in dangerous situations. And they just as often meet such an ignoble end at the hands of men who leave no evidence for us to follow."

"There is evidence, Morley, there's the boot print."

"Which is compelling, but not absolute. Any number of men could have left that print, and it'll be difficult to use something like that to convict in court."

Mercy scowled at him. "You're acting as though you're preparing me for her murder to never be solved."

"That's exactly what I'm doing."

His answer paralyzed her. Morley got to where he was by nabbing and convicting more murderers than anyone in the history of Scotland Yard.

"How could you say that?" she accused.

His gesture was cajoling as he placed a warm hand on her forearm. "We are stretched so thin, Mercy. I'm endeavoring to hire more officers, but detectives are difficult to come by. There is a rise in gang violence be- cause the substances of the streets have spilled into the solariums of the wealthy and powerful. I'm putting down migrant riots and trade strikes. We're in the middle of a crime wave, and I'm doing my utmost to keep hundreds of women and children who are still alive, that way."

"What are you saying?" Aghast, she stepped out of

his reach. "That the murder of one measly drunken socialite doesn't merit investigation? Do you agree with Trout when he said Mathilde isn't worth the trouble it would take to find her justice?"

"Of course not." Morley ran frustrated fingers through his hair, tugging as if to pull a solution out of it. "I'm saying an investigation like this is rarely simple and almost never timely. We will do what we can for Mrs. Archambeau, you have my word. In fact, this is just the sort of case the Knight of Shadows takes interest in, eh?"

He gave her a friendly nudge to the shoulder.

Mercy nodded, more to get rid of him than anything.

"Let this go, Mercy. Let justice take its course."

The Knight of Shadows was an effective vigilante, to be sure, but no one knew how to contact him. He was a man. He did what he liked.

Oh, she'd let justice take its course...

Because justice, as everyone knew, was a woman.

CHAPTER 8

"*H*ow did this happen?"

Raphael knew to expect the question, but he never ceased to flinch upon its asking.

Because it produced a maelstrom of emotion he couldn't escape.

Guilt. Shame. Pain. Hatred.

Most of *all*, hatred.

Less toward the men who had done this to his brother, than the one who had brokered it.

He still seethed.

Grappled rage into submission as he watched Dr. Titus Conleith palpate his brother's ruined face for the final examination before tomorrow's reconstructive surgery.

Raphael detested everything about hospitals, though this one was nicer than most.

The glaring awful whiteness of them, the smell of solutions and cleansers. Of shit and blood and food and death. Even the neatness of them rankled. Rows of beds full of misery. Nurses dressed in smart uniforms, their hair held in severe knots beneath starched caps.

It made him all the more determined to die whilst young and healthy.

Gabriel was the only soul alive that could get him through these doors.

If his brother could suffer such indignities, the least Raphael could do was be there.

He only had to watch.

They had visited Dr. Conleith several times in the past handful of weeks, and never once had the surgeon savant made the dreaded query.

How did this happen?

How did Gabriel come to be without a large portion of his nose? How was it that his ocular bone had split so completely as to cave in, leaving him unable to properly open his left eye? How had the skin of his cheek ripped all the way through, from the corner of his mouth to his temple, only to be stitched together by a drunken hack?

"Violence." Sitting on the surgeon's examination table, Gabriel gave the same short answer he always did. The truth, and yet...

Not all of it. Not even close.

The memory—*memories* were Raphael's absolute worst.

And it hadn't even happened to him.

The violence.

Dr. Conleith reached for the stark-white-bulbed lamp, pulling it closer to Gabriel's face. It illuminated the macabre smile crafted by the tight, uneven line of the scar branching from the corner of his mouth to his hairline.

Raphael could barely stand to look at it, even after all these years.

He wanted to strike the handsome doctor for pointing such glaring lights on the ancient wounds when he knew how it distressed his brother. His fingers itched to bloody the stern brow that furrowed with pity as he bent over Gabriel's expressionless, long-suffering face.

It was the tension bulging his brother's muscles and the trickle of sweat running from his shorn scalp into the back of his collar that brought out the instinct to break the doctor's strong jaw as it flexed and released, as if chewing on a thought.

Must it be so light in here?

They visited under the cover of night so as not to be so thusly exposed.

As if he could instinctively sense the rage simmering right beneath Raphael's skin, the doctor glanced over to where he lingered by an articulated skeleton, holding the wall up with his shoulder.

To Conleith's credit, he didn't seem cowed by the brothers Sauvageau in the least. "I ask not out of morbid curiosity, but occupational necessity," he explained with his very professional brand of patience. "It appears to me that some of these wounds sustained subsequent trauma, which makes my job a great deal more difficult."

Subsequent trauma, what a gentle way to put it.

Neither he nor Gabriel answered.

Dr. Conleith rubbed at his close-cropped beard, one with a more russet hue than his tidy brown hair. "Answer me this, then. In regard to the ocular cavity, this was done by an instrument, I suspect?"

"It was."

"Blunt or sharp-edged?"

"Sharp." Gabriel's words were often difficult to mark. His voice hailed from lower in a chest deeper than most men could boast. Protected by dense ribs and muscles built upon what seemed to be other muscle, the register was often so low as to be lost.

The reason they often created the fiction that Gabriel couldn't speak or understand English was twofold. One, because people spoke more freely around someone who might not mark them.

And the other, because speaking caused Gabriel discomfort.

The stitching done to his mouth and cheek had been of such terrible design, it'd taken the ability to part his lips very well without fear of tearing the wound anew.

"So sharp, but not as sharp as the instrument that tore the cheek open, is that correct?" The doctor used his thumbs to lift the lip up toward the exposed nasal cavity.

Gabriel, a man who'd undergone more pain than even Raphael could imagine, gave a grunt of discomfort.

Raphael pushed away from the wall, taking a threatening step toward the doctor, who'd turned his back.

His brother held out a staying hand, planting Raphael's feet to the floor.

"I'm sorry for any discomfort," the doctor said gently as he released Gabriel's face and stepped away to wash his hands. "I was testing the elasticity of the skin."

"It was lumber."

Conleith turned around, his hands frozen with suds, as if he'd not heard Gabriel correctly. "Pardon?"

Raphael's mouth dropped open in astonishment. They never spoke of it. To anyone.

Ever.

"Long and square cut." Gabriel stretched his arms out wide to show the length of the wood that had caved his face in. "The kind used to build houses. Does that...change anything? Will you still be able to operate?"

Though Gabriel was his elder brother, larger in every respect, Raphael felt such a swell of protectiveness, he swallowed around a gather of emotion lodged in his throat, threatening to cut off his breath. Not even when they'd been young had he spoken with such uncertainty. With such hope and dread laced into one inquiry.

"Of course." The doctor answered in his quick and clipped tone. "Without question." He turned back to the sink to finish scrubbing his hands.

From his vantage, Raphael watched the doctor work diligently to school the aching compassion out of his expression.

It was appreciated.

Conleith obviously knew enough about men to realize that those who led a life such as theirs equated compassion with pity.

Pity was an insult.

And insults were answered.

Must have learned that in the Afghan war, where he'd earned his hard-won reputation by reportedly stitching together men even more broken than his brother.

Though that was hard to believe.

"Explain to me, Doctor, why you must put Gabriel through more than one procedure. This wouldn't be to make it seem as if the fortune we allowed you and your wife to keep was worth the trouble..."

The seams of the midnight-blue shirt strained over Gabriel's shoulder as he lifted his arm to jam a finger in Raphael's direction. "Do not intimidate the doctor," he commanded in their heavily accented French.

Raphael made a rude gesture and answered him in kind. "Does he look intimidated to you?"

The man was in no danger, and not only because he was the only surgeon who could perform such procedures in this country, but because he was married to Mercy's beloved eldest sister.

The idea of doing anything to cause her pain produced an ache in his own body.

"It's a valid question." Conleith strode to the skeleton held upon a post next to Raphael, whose nose looked alarmingly like his brother's. "Since your wounds have been healed for years, I'll need to re-break some of the bone in your cheek and then use a panel of sorts to sculpt it back together per a foundational technique pioneered by the Italian doctor, Gasparo Tagliacozzi." He showed on the skull where the break would occur and where the panel would be fitted. "I certainly have reason to hope that this will help with the terrible headaches you're plagued with. However, the procedure is new and complicated and could take several hours. I shouldn't like you to be anesthetized much longer than that, the risk of you not...regaining consciousness is too high."

Gabriel's chin dipped once. "I understand."

"Subsequently, Dr. Karl Ferdinand von Gräfe has shown me how to take skin from another part of your body, and not only shape you an entirely new nose, but also cut open your badly healed scar tissue and graft it so you will be able to speak and chew more easily."

"Where will the skin be taken from?" Gabriel attempting to furrow his brow was a terrible thing to behold.

More ghastly than normal, in any case.

The doctor hesitated. "Usually from the arm, but because of your tattoos, we'll have to take it from your back."

"All right, Doctor." His brother stood, and it still surprised Raphael to note that Conleith was every bit as tall as the towering gangster, if only three fourths as wide.

Not that Titus Conleith was a diminutive man. Indeed, he was strenuously fit, but Gabriel should have been named Goliath. Or Ajax.

As he'd the proportions not often seen on a mortal.

"Tomorrow night, then." Rather than offering his hand, Gabriel nodded to the doctor, who seemed to understand that he'd rather dispense with the pleasantries.

He turned away from any sort of audience as he affixed the black mask over his features. It stayed put by way of a strap that encircled the shorn crown of his head like the band of a hat, and settled down over the left side of his features with a frightening, if familiar, prosthetic shape of a man's face.

It always reminded Raphael of someone attempting to break free of a black marble statue.

After, Gabriel donned his long black coat, drawing up the hood to hide as much of himself as possible.

The observant doctor bustled around, rolling his shirtsleeves down his forearms and affixing the cufflinks to allow them the semblance of privacy. "I like my patients to bathe and scrub as clean as possible and also to forgo meals the day of a procedure, if possible," he said. "Sometimes the anesthetic can cause nausea, and I shouldn't like you to aspirate whilst asleep."

With these last few words, he opened the door to their private room—a courtesy not afforded to many patients, no doubt—and escorted them out the door and into the night.

Both brothers enjoyed a simultaneous inhale of crisp February air as they melted into the familiar darkness of the streets.

They'd always been creatures of the shadows.

But perhaps not for much longer.

"For a moment there, I thought you were going to tell him about the pits," Raphael prompted. "About everything."

It wasn't cold enough to lift his collar to shield him, but Gabriel did it anyway as he ignored any mention of the pits. "The two procedures will set everything back. We'll need to make other arrangements."

"I'm not worried." Raphael lifted his shoulder and watched the billow of his breath break as he walked into it. "What are a few more days? No one will be looking for us."

Since Raphael couldn't read his brother's expressions, he'd learned to pick up on other cues, some as subtle as mere vibrations in the air between them.

The set of his boulder-sized shoulders, the number of times he cracked his knuckles, as he was wont to do when brooding. "I still don't know if we can pull this off without bodies to confirm our deaths."

Raphael elbowed his brother, feinting at shoving him into a gas lamppost. "Find me a body that could pass for yours, and I'll gleefully murder him and enjoy pretending it's you."

Gabriel didn't even pretend to be amused. "It is hard for me, knowing I will not be awake to oversee things."

Clutching at his heart, Raphael acted as though he'd been skewered. "Your lack of trust wounds me, brother. Fatally, I expect. I should not have to fake my death."

"Keep your voice down," Gabriel snarled, searching the empty night for interlopers.

The Fauves didn't haunt this part of town.

Sobering, Raphael rested his palm on Gabriel's shoulder, the one from which the real mantle of leadership rested.

As the face of the Fauves, Raphael was an effective figurehead. Sleek and elegant, dangerously charismatic, cunning, and collected.

And, admittedly, not difficult to look at.

But few knew that he was the tip of the blade wielded by his brother.

Gabriel wasn't just muscle, as most suspected, he was might.

He was master.

Because of the rules by which they'd always lived.

The rules they now carefully planned to leave behind.

"I have it well in hand, brother." Raphael squeezed the tense muscle before releasing it, wishing he could say more.

Wishing he had more time with the only person he loved in this world.

Gabriel's chest expanded with another measured breath. "Tell me again."

"Once you are recovered enough to travel, you will retrieve your new papers from Frank Walters and go to the Indies. I have transferred our enormous fortune to St. John's Bank in Switzerland, where I will retrieve it. After, we will meet in Antigua and from there go to America using our new identities."

"You'll telegraph the villa if something goes awry," Gabriel reminded him unnecessarily.

"That goes without saying, even though you've said it twenty times too many."

A grunt from his brother was as close as he ever came to a laugh.

"The extra days will serve us well," Raphael continued. "It gives me time to make the arrangements to have Mathilde's ashes go with us. We can spread them from the Brooklyn Bridge. She'd like that, I think."

Gabriel's gait changed, which was how Raphael knew he was about to say something that made him uncomfortable. "I know she was difficult... but I am sorry Mathilde is gone."

"As am I."

They fell silent as they stopped at the back-garden gate of the mansion no one knew they occupied. Their fountain tinkled in the background, mingling with the sounds of an approaching couple.

Raphael thought back to the day when his father had told them that the only way to escape their destiny was death.

Well...turned out the bastard had been right.

As the couple approached, the man deftly moved his lady to the opposite side of the walk, placing himself between Gabriel's bulk and her body.

Though they were in the part of the West End that was well patrolled, and where street ruffians rarely dared to venture, it was Gabriel's bulk and general air of menace that ignited the man's protective instinct.

Besides that move, the pair paid them little mind as they swished by, chattering as if nothing could touch them in the infatuated world they'd created.

Raphael would not have even marked them, if not for his brother.

Gabriel watched them with undue intensity. His fingers twitched as the man ran his hand along the woman's face.

Shifting uncomfortably, Raphael second-guessed his own plans for the evening.

All he'd desired in the hours since he'd left Mercy's side, was to return to it. Once the sun had gone down, he'd been nearly vibrating out of his skin with anticipation.

Walking around half hard at the thought of having her, hoping no one would notice.

Especially his brother, who had never so much as touched a woman.

He'd been born and bred a machine of violence. And nothing more.

Where would Gabriel fit in this world when they were through? He knew nothing else.

He *was* nothing else.

Raphael thumped Gabriel's chest to catch his attention. "Don't be worried, yeah? The doctor said that big dolts like you don't die in surgery often."

"I'm not nervous."

"Then what is wrong with you?"

His neck swiveled back to the woman. "Nothing."

Raphael took in a gigantic breath, bracing himself for extreme disappointment. He wanted Mercy with an ache he'd never known, but on an evening as momentous as this, he should be there for his brother.

"Do you want company?" he asked. "Let's get a round, yeah?"

"Not tonight." Gabriel fished his pipe out of his pocket and packed it with an expensive tobacco he was fond of. "I'm going to check a few things."

That brought Raphael to attention. "What things?"

"Never you mind."

Raphael rolled his eyes. There was no talking to him when he was like this. "Well, I'll be off then."

He pointed his shoes in the direction of Cresthaven Place.

"What are you about tonight?" Gabriel asked, as if it had only just occurred to him to do so.

"Never *you* mind." Raphael threw the answer over his shoulder.

"Raphael Thierry Sauvageau." His brother's glare was an uncomfortable prickle along his spine, so he turned to face it.

"I'm *going* for a woman, if you must know, you insufferable nag." They'd always japed and jibed and poked at each other. Gabriel knew he had women. That he was somewhat a lothario, but they never really discussed it.

It had always seemed insensitive to do so.

Tonight, it felt especially so.

He put out a hand. "Gabriel, I'm sorry. I—"

"Don't be." The words were released into the night like a puff of smoke over gravel.

Impatience warred with guilt in Raphael's chest. "Why don't you just put on an entire mask and pay some strumpet to at least suck your—"

"*Go*, Rafe."

He put his hands up. Feeling both awful and relieved.

Were he making any other decision regarding his own future, he'd have insisted they abide.

Were his life expected to be any longer than a couple of nights... he'd have spent it all gladly with his brother.

But Gabriel had been right about one thing. The men of the underworld—and the officers of the law—would never believe them truly dead without a body to identify.

And that body would be his.

Gabriel had never lived a life before, and Raphael had devoured whatever he could from his own existence.

Now, he'd the opportunity to give his brother a second chance.

But first...Raphael would taste a bit of heaven before hell claimed his restless soul.

Mercy Goode would be the name on his lips. Nay, the taste lingering on his tongue when he met his death at the Midwinter Masquerade.

CHAPTER 9

It wasn't a noise that woke Mercy.

But her body.

It came alive, rousing her from restless, wicked dreams. Banishing them from memory the moment her eyes flew open.

And found Raphael Sauvageau silhouetted against her window.

The wispy white drapes stirred around him, reaching as if disturbed by a shade, or by the very potency of his atmosphere as he stood.

Watching her.

The light of the lone lamp she'd left burning painted shadows on his face, casting one single expression in both stark and savage relief.

Hunger.

She remained burrowed to the neck beneath her plush blue blankets, shivering not only with cold, but with vulnerability.

One look from him threatened to strip her bare. Expose her in ways she'd not prepared for.

He'd come for his pound of flesh.

He'd come to claim her.

Mercy cast about for something erudite and

worldly to say, some greeting that a temptress, a lover, would tantalize him with.

"Erm—hullo."

Well...Shelley she was not.

"I was going to let you sleep." His voice rumbled into the air of her room with a foreign vibration, splashing against her nerves with all the threat of thunder in the great distance.

A man had never entered this room, certainly not at night.

"I wasn't sleeping." She yawned against the back of her knuckles.

"Oh?" He drifted inside, shutting the window behind him.

Locking them in together.

"Do you often snore whilst awake?"

"I don't snore," she protested.

A smile toyed with the corner of his mouth, though he didn't argue the point. "Forgive me for being tardy. I had urgent business with my brother to attend, and it took longer than I hoped. An eternity, in fact. When I knew you were here. Waiting."

"You weren't tardy, as I didn't know when to expect you." She would have shrugged if she were not curled on her side, swaddled in a pile of blankets. "If I'm honest, I expected a messenger at first. I thought it would be tidier to meet somewhere other than Cresthaven, where we might be discovered."

He conducted a quick study of her room, the rich blue accents contrasting with clean white walls gentled by gilded paintings and tapestries. "Here is as safe as any place. Your parents are not in residence and your sister is in the next room fast asleep."

Should she be disconcerted or impressed that he knew that? "Might someone be roused if...if we make noise?"

His eyes flared as he approached her bed, but he made no move to join her upon it. Instead, he crossed his arms and propped his shoulder on her tall bedpost.

If he was dangerously handsome in the sunlight, at night he was utterly fatal.

The darkness embraced him as a creature of its own. Blessed him with satirical beauty and fiendish grace.

He was a demon in a bespoke suit.

"You are so open," he noted. "So straightforward and bold. There isn't a hint of coyness or artifice about you."

A defensiveness welled in her chest. "I don't know how to be coy and I don't have time for artifice. Besides, why are women expected to be shy or tentative? Why must the fact that I am bold or inquisitive be revolutionary?"

"I was admiring, not admonishing. I find everything about you refreshing. Alluring."

"Oh... well... thank you." Mercy chewed on her lip, trying to figure out a way for them to *not* say anything further. The longer men spoke with her, the more likely she was to drive them away.

"Why don't you undress and get in?" she ventured, tucking back a section of the covers.

He made a sound of disbelief deep in his throat. "You want me to undress here? In front of you?" He uncrossed his arms and lowered them to his sides, regarding her with a wicked scrutiny. "Are you a voyeur, Mercy Goode?"

"I don't know what I am," she answered honestly. "But you can't get in bed with your shoes on. Nor can we—accomplish our aim—while you're dressed, I expect."

"Accomplish our aim?" His mouth flattened with chagrin. "Is that what we're calling it?"

The tips of her ears began to burn again, she ducked her head under the covers. "Don't make me say the word while I'm looking at you."

His chuckle was like the purr of a tiger and washed her in prickles of awareness, pebbling the tips of her nipples. "How can you do the deed if you cannot speak the word?"

He made an excellent point, though she'd die before telling him so. "Fornicate," she spat from beneath the coverlet. "Now could you take off your clothes and join me please?"

This time his laughter was genuine and rich. She shivered with pleasure at being the one to have produced it.

Even if it was at her expense.

She peeked out at him.

Bucking away from the bedpost, he blinked at her from beneath dark, suggestive lashes. "Oftentimes, lovers undress each other."

"Oh..." She struggled into a seated position, clutching the sheets to her unbound breasts. "Well, I undressed myself so you wouldn't have to."

Raphael closed his eyes for a moment and brought his fist to his mouth where his teeth sank into a knuckle.

Suddenly uncertain, Mercy asked, "Should I not have done? Do you want me to put my nightdress back on so you can be the one—?"

"No!" He cleared his throat. Inhaled. Exhaled. And tried again. "No... I will undress and join you there. Keep the damned covers on or I'll not be able to contain myself."

"I shouldn't think you're here to contain yourself, rather the opposite," she teased.

"For a woman's first time, a man should *always* contain himself." He said this as if lecturing himself.

She didn't know enough about it to disagree with him.

The sight of Raphael's deft fingers undoing the knot at his collar did something wicked to her insides. All her boldness deserted her as he undid the buttons of his shirt and vest, shucking them down his shoulders.

Mercy's eyes widened at the sight of his tattoos. Black ink danced and swirled over his tawny skin, rising over broad, round shoulders and circled down one corded arm. They were a chaotic array of blasphemies. A religious icon inked adjacent to a naked woman in a suggestive pose. A raven perched on a skull. Other beasts interspersed with pagan symbols and words or verse in his native language.

One thing became instantly obvious. He was the art...the depictions were merely decorations.

The disks of his chest were smooth, unfettered by hair or adornment, and sloped down to the slight corrugations of his ribs and the deep etchings of abdominal muscles.

The only hair she could see, aside from his head, was a dark line disappearing into his trousers.

He undressed without hurrying, watching her watch him.

Touching her, all of her, without touching her at all.

His hands rested at the placket of buttons beneath which the barrel of a bulge nudged to be uncovered.

Mercy almost swallowed her tongue. Should she be anxious?

Was she?

Raphael paused long enough for her to take in a breath. "Have you ever seen a naked man before?"

She forced herself to drag her eyes back to his. "Of course, I have."

His dark brow arched as darker questions emerged upon a growl. "When? Who?"

"Well... there's David, of course, and various other statuary. I mean, Achilles is right there in Hyde Park for all to see."

He seemed to relax, and when he looked at her, his eyes swam with limitless tenderness.

"There was also a medical text Felicity and I found in Titus's office. We studied that *most* thoroughly. I know all there is to know about the male anatomy...medically speaking."

A soft catch in his throat could have been a laugh, but he schooled his features admirably.

"But never...in the flesh?" he clarified.

That word. *Flesh.* It made her tingle.

She didn't *want* to be untried. Couldn't bring herself to admit her inexperience in front of a man who likely knew all there was regarding what they were about to do.

And so, to retreat from answering an uncomfortable question that would leave her open to his derision, she found herself babbling.

Starting a conversation.

At a time like *this*.

And actively hating herself as she did so.

"I wanted to tell you...I exonerated you to Chief Inspector Morley. Scotland Yard is no longer after you—well—for Mathilde's murder, at least."

"Oh?" His hands remained hooked in his waistband and made no move at all.

"He seemed convinced as I that you didn't do it."

"I suppose I owe you my gratitude, Detective Goode." He smiled down at her.

"I showed him the sort of boots that left the print and... I drew diagrams." *Stop talking, you ninny*, she ordered herself. Or he'll never undo his trousers. "I was thinking perhaps tomorrow night we could both go to the Midwinter Masquerade, see who we can question regarding Mathilde."

Lord, but she was bungling this.

She should have guessed that she would.

His hands fell away from his trousers. "You're not going to the masquerade."

"I don't recall asking your permission."

"I don't recall mentioning to you where it was being held."

For once, she bit her tongue.

Mathilde had informed her where it was being held, but *he* needn't know that.

"Mercy." He went to the bed and sat on it, taking one of her hands and allowing the other to keep her modesty, such as it was. "Women like you don't belong at the Midwinter Masquerade. You'd regret it if you went."

"I'm not an idiot. You needn't threaten me."

"I'm warning you. It's not a savory affair. Surely you know that."

"Everyone knows that," she said with a droll look. "Are you going to be there?"

"If I were to attend, I might not be around long enough to make certain you're safe."

"Why not?"

For the first time, he couldn't seem to meet her gaze. "If you find anything else out about the case, do not follow up on it yourself. Go to the authorities. To Morley."

"But—"

"Please?"

She sighed...wondering if this man had ever begged another human being in his entire life.

She phrased her reply with the utmost care. "I will go to Morley with anything additional I learn about the case." *After the Midnight Masquerade*, she amended silently. She was no retiring debutante who needed her delicate sensibilities protected along with her reputation. She knew better than to be alone with any of the reprobates who would surely attend. But it was the last plan Mathilde had ever made. She owed it to the woman to seek the truth there.

He raised her hand to his lips, kissing the back of her knuckles. "I consider it a personal favor."

"You're going to leave tonight," she realized aloud. Of course, that's what he'd been referring to when he said he would not be around. They weren't proper lovers. This was no affair of the heart. He'd made certain to let her know that, even during his proposition.

Would you let me fuck you, Mercy Goode?

He said nothing about caring or cuddling.

Staying.

He would fuck her and then... What? Thank her promptly and dress?

Even sitting, he towered like some Roman god, skin like honey poured over steel.

And frozen with an aghast expression on his face.

"Not that I'm expecting you to stay," she rushed on in one breath, attempting to appear nonchalant. "I am aware that such liaisons are conducted without much ceremony or expectation, and I wanted you to be comfortable knowing that you'll get none from me. We shall...do what it is we're here to do and take what— several minutes at least? Though I've heard it can be as brief as—"

He'd covered his mouth with his hand, but he couldn't hide the shake in his shoulders or the creases of mirth at the corner of his eyes.

"You're laughing," she accused, incensed. "Is this funny to you?"

"Don't be irate with me, *mon chaton*. I scoff only at the idea of a brief encounter between us."

She knew she looked churlish, but she was trying to decide whether she believed him or not.

His eyes became pools of liquid desire. "With you I intend to take my time. I will make it last until the tolling of the bells warn of the dawn."

Her thighs quivered. "Oh. Well...I'll admit that I prefer that. It seems silly for you to come all this way if you're only going to take all of a few minutes."

"The home I share with Gabriel is not so far." He gestured to the west. "But I would have dragged myself through Siberia in winter to be here tonight."

At this, she smiled, feeling uncharacteristically shy by his unabashed appreciation of her.

"I'm glad," she murmured. "That we desire each other with equal fervor."

Oh, *now* what had she said that was funny?

"Darling," he managed over his mirth. "If you wanted me like I wanted you, we'd be on our second time by now."

"Oh. Well..." Not to be outdone in the surprise seduction, she dropped her sheets and let them pool in a white cloud at her waist.

The laughter died with a groan in his throat.

He didn't just look at her. He consumed the sight of her with an ardent fervor.

"You are stunning, Mercy," he marveled. "Exceptional. You never cease to astonish me."

"What do I do that is so surprising?" she wondered aloud.

"Most women would at least make modest, maidenly protestations. Force me to coax them to reveal themselves to me."

"Most women are trained to act like simpering fools," she scoffed. "Is that what you want from me?" She pressed the back of her hand to her forehead, enjoying that he watched how her breasts lifted with the gesture. "Oh, do allow me a moment to swoon here in virginal protestation so I might feel less guilty for succumbing to the seduction of this large and dangerous rogue who is intent upon ravishing my pure and virtuous person. I am an innocent, harmless girl caught in his dastardly web—"

His unexpected touch at her throat seized her breath there.

Her heart skipped a beat, then two, paralyzed as his strong fingers trailed to the back of her neck, pressing deeper against the tight, quivering muscles there.

"In my experience, women are generally arousing or amusing, I'm delighted that you are both."

"I amuse you?"

"You transfix me, Mercy. You captivate me."

With deft and clever circles, he found the tender knots in her back and undid them with steady, circling pressure.

He did this to relax her, and it was working.

And...not working.

The strength in his hands was both potent and restrained. She found the dichotomy endlessly erotic.

Hypnotic, even.

Her blood thickened. Slowed to a heavy languor as if warm honey drenched her veins with sweet, treacle sensuality.

Probably she should compliment him, as well. He certainly deserved it.

"You also...intrigue...*Oh*, that feels so good," she groaned and closed her eyes in bliss as he found a tender spot and curled his relentless fingers into it.

"Just you wait, *mon chaton*," he promised against her ear. "Do not be too easily satisfied. I like a challenge."

She couldn't summon the words with which to reply. Not only because of what his diabolical fingers did to her, or the way his words made her heart quiver instead of beat.

But because a wave of aching emotion tumbled over her, swamping her with unidentifiable yearning. Not just for the carnal sensations his touch evoked, but for this affection between them.

This physical touch that was not demanding nor expectant.

Unhurried. Deliberate. Both intimate and innocuous all at once.

She sighed as he released her tresses from their pins, lock by spiraling lock, testing the weight and coil of the curl as if he'd never before threaded fingers through a woman's hair.

Or never would again.

After a while, he said, "Though you jested before, there is truth in what you said. One you must consider carefully. I am a large and dangerous man... My web is one of deceit and blood."

"I knew that already. I'm not blind."

"No." He leaned forward, brushing the ghost of a kiss against each of her eyelids. "You have excellent, beautiful eyes. You see what most do not."

"Your flattery will get you nowhere, you cad." She reached out, shocked when her hand encountered the warm flesh of his chest.

Shocked that she kept it there, searching for the beat of a heart she could never claim.

"I'm already where I want to be." The earnestness of his expression unstitched her as he reached his own palm out, and pressed it to where her own heart hurled itself against the cage of her chest.

"What do you feel when I touch you?" His voice washed her in a pleasant glow, the question putting her at ease. "When you touch me?"

"Butterflies," she answered honestly, placing her other hand over where wings made a riot in her belly.

He tilted his head, his hand moving lower, not to her breast quite yet, but almost. "Butterflies? Don't they erupt when you are afraid?"

"I'm not afraid," she lied.

"What are you?"

"Excited."

"Excitement is often born of fear."

But was fear also this delicious? She wondered.

Her silence seemed to consternate him. "Is that why you relented to my wicked proposition? Am I your one chance to dance with danger?" His hand stilled as he gazed at her. "Will you regret saying yes to me when this is over?"

"Certainly not." Her eyes flew open and she drew back, an offended frown tugging at the corners of her lips. "I said yes because you're the one man who makes me feel more alive by just walking into a room. I said yes because I was categorically certain I'd regret it if I refused this opportunity for pleasure."

His eyes gleamed like those of a night-hunting predator beneath a moonless sky.

She'd the sense she'd just disconcerted him.

Oh dear, had she been too honest again?

This time, when his fingers dug into the back of her neck, it was to drag her forward and slant his lips over hers.

She melted into him like wax beneath a flame, surrendering and puddling in the fire he ignited.

Dragging his tongue against hers, he licked and tasted, his breath coming in rasping pants. Feral, guttural noises vibrated across her lips, into her mouth, and down to the very core of her.

His hands wandered, the skin rough and the movements gentle.

He seemed to understand her impatience. To craft it, mirror it, and then ignore it, drawing out some delicious distraction with a swirl of his tongue or a barely-there nip of his teeth.

She could kiss him forever, but it wasn't enough. She desired him closer. Over her, beneath her. Beside her.

Inside her.

He wanted her, too, dammit, so why didn't he just—?

As if he'd heard her thoughts, he was suddenly above her. Settling his weight between her parted thighs, he kept the sheet and his trousers between them.

His lean hips kicked forward, introducing her to the hard length of his arousal as he fed the fire of their kiss until it threatened to scorch her.

Mercy couldn't tell if he'd uttered the ragged moan or she had.

Dangerous thoughts filtered through her consciousness as he caressed her in places she hadn't expected. He drew knuckles across her jaw, and she imagined devotion in his touch. He feathered caresses across her clavicles and ghosted his palms down bare shoulders.

She might have found a pledge whispered on the pants of his breath.

Impossible.

Even in the darkness, she could sense the pace of his heart, hammering with a tempo as furious and drastic as her own.

He dragged his lips from hers after a moment, making a moist trail with his mouth up the line of her jaw.

It wasn't his lust that amazed her, it was his tenderness. His lips quested across her hairline, temple, and down the nape of her neck. He took in deep drags of breath, as if he could lock the scent of her inside of him.

"Mine." His head dipped low enough, the word caressed her throat, chased by lips that stopped to sample the tender skin and tease the sensitive nerves there.

Her entire being trembled in expectant anticipation of his touch, of the shivery whisper of his warm breath a moment before his lips followed.

"You are an incomparable beauty." He said this like an accusation, before his mouth found her breast and began an erotic assault upon it that left her utterly defenseless. He deprived her of air, of thought, of any sort of reason as he held her immobile beneath him. Some of his tenderness seemed to abandon him now, as he licked and nipped at her with intensifying aggression.

Her body bloomed for it. She knew what making love entailed. The mechanics of the act, at least. But she'd been truly unprepared for this instinctive urgency.

This assault of sensation.

How did anyone bear it?

She barely noticed his shift in weight until the slide of the sheet became a torturous shiver down her body as he drew it away from her.

He stretched on his side next to her, freeing his hand to explore the skin he'd uncovered with carnal strokes.

When he turned to look at what he'd exposed to the lamplight, Mercy seized each side of his jaw with both hands and imprisoned his mouth to hers.

She'd thought she was ready to be naked.

But not to be revealed.

He didn't protest as she plunged her tongue into his mouth, tasting his need, sweeping in the rhythm of her growing desire.

A clever finger traced inside her thigh, petted

through soft intimate hair, dashing erotic sparkles of sensation over her entire body.

Her breath froze as he delved into bare, wet flesh. Her pulse didn't just run, it fled, escaping her as he slid unhurried explorations through sensitized ruffles of feminine skin.

He broke the seal of their lips, moaning something in French she was too mindless to translate.

She melted—liquified—beneath his expert touch. She marveled at the slippery warmth of her own body's response to him. Wondered if she should be ashamed. Or embarrassed.

Too entranced to bother with either.

She felt drugged with some throbbing intoxicant. It dragged her into a miasma of pleasure and threatened to drown her beneath turbulent, ocean-deep waves of sensation.

Languid explorations tightened to circles around the place where a shimmer of heat threatened to become a firestorm. His increasingly urgent breaths crashed against her mouth as he lingered upon the threat of a kiss, but kept his mouth enticingly elusive.

She clutched at him, with her fingers and with—Oh, God—the spasming intimate muscles of her sex as he drew a teasing circle around the entrance to her body.

A gasp closed her throat as he nudged gently there, and she stilled, not realizing until this very moment just how desperately she desired him inside of her.

"I want to taste you," he growled. "Would you let me?"

"Yes," she said impatiently, tugging at his shoulders to bring their lips back together. "Yes, of course. *Please.*"

His chuckle was demonic. "I like it when you beg."

"I was *not* beggi—where are you going?"

He prowled down her body, wide shoulders rolling like a great cat as he did so. His nose and lips stopped to sample at her scent, and then nibble at soft and tender parts of her.

Her clavicles.

The undersides of her breasts.

The gently rounded plane of her belly.

"You're clever, Inspector Goode, I'm sure you have some clue as to where I'm headed."

The very thought made her nearly apoplectic, but she dug her fingers into the sheets so as not to stop him out of sheer humiliation.

"I thought you meant to kiss me," she clarified.

His laugh would have made the devil shudder. "Oh, but I *do*. I mean to kiss you thoroughly."

"But...but..." *There?* She squeezed her thighs shut as his lips trailed the short downy distance from her belly button to the triangle of dark gold hair below.

"Everywhere." His hands nudged her wobbly legs open, and she nearly gave in to the instinct to protest.

She'd heard of the French being more wicked than the average lover, but this was beyond the pale. Wasn't it? Or at least unhygienic...

Did he really mean to—?

Crisp air feathered across the wet heat between her parted legs. His fingers, firm and competent, pinned her thighs all the way open, utterly exposing her to him.

"Look at you," he whispered, his words landing *there*. Against her most intimate parts. "Magnificent. I should have expected..."

Expected what? She wanted to ask.

Would have asked.

Had he not done exactly what he promised, and kissed her.

The shock of his hot wet mouth against her warm wet sex... She never could have imagined the contrast of it. The pure illicit pleasure it evoked.

She felt those lips everywhere.

Or perhaps her entire world simply faded to only contain what his mouth currently did to her.

All she knew was the heat of his breath.

The slick velvet of his tongue.

The gentle coaxing of his lips.

Mercy looked down the topography of her body as if such an act needed a witness.

Their eyes locked, and she thought of the serpent again—especially as his tongue flicked and slithered in gentle pulses over her most sensitive flesh.

The light burnished him in stark relief, his shoulders so corded and wide against the thin white skin of her limbs. His arms, so densely muscled, held her a willing hostage as he consumed her like a condemned man might his final meal.

The peaks of her breasts were drawn into tight, aching beads, and without thought, she cupped one. Hoping to warm it, to soothe some strange throbbing there.

The groan he emitted vibrated through her loins and drew a surge of bliss into a threatening crest. His lips never left her sex, sealed to her with a rhythmic suction that created subtle, shadowed hollows in his cheeks.

It was the bliss on his features that transfixed her. The rhythmic undulations of his hips against the counterpane where he sprawled. The deep sounds of pleasure she felt in her very bones.

He enjoyed this.

A storm built below his mouth. Swirling in the movements of his tongue.

The thunder was no longer in the distance.

No, it was inside of her. Rolling and pulsing and deeply erotic.

Tears stung her lids. She was suddenly unprepared

for something so profound. So powerful it threatened to tear her away from herself.

So inevitable, she knew she could not fight it.

That it would not stop.

"Raphael?" She whimpered his name for the first time.

His gaze found hers, his pupils so dilated his eyes looked demon black.

"What is—? I don't—I'm—I'm—" Though a sort of feverish delirium, she couldn't bring herself to finish the sentences she desperately needed him to hear.

What is going to happen?

I don't know what to do.

I'm lost.

He didn't stop. He didn't hesitate, slow, or even pause.

But his eyes contained a sincere sort of understanding, and he released her thigh to slide his hand—palm up—across the sheet at her side.

She grasped at his offer of salvation the very instant she was pitched over the cliff.

And she'd never been more grateful for anything as she was for the curl of his strong fingers around hers.

Mercy dangled between solid ground and air for an intense and breathless eternity before plummeting into a writhing, delirious, free-fall of ecstasy.

The strokes of his tongue became lashes of lightning-hot pleasure bolting through her blood, suffusing her with electric charges that ebbed for a moment of answering thunder. She needn't have worried about making noise, as she couldn't produce a single sound as the storm tore the breath from her lungs.

She writhed and thrashed with uninhibited euphoria. One moment grinding into it, and the next retreating from it.

As if by magic, Raphael seemed to realize when it

became too much, when the pleasure threatened to shatter her on the rocks below.

The strokes gentled then, becoming cajoling and reverent, like a prayer or some such profane thing. He drew out the last spasms from her core with sinuous skill until she utterly collapsed.

Even though he'd destroyed her with pleasure, Raphael still picked over the wreckage of her body with thorough, searching little nips and licks. Reanimating her boneless, corpse-like torpor with little twitches and trembles of aftershocks.

When she made a helpless, plaintive noise, he finally relented, pulling away with a wet and depraved sound.

Releasing her hand, he rolled away and stood, wiping the slick leavings of her from his lips with the back of his hand as he kicked off his shoes.

She wanted to clutch at him, to call him back, and felt so pathetic for the impulse, she forced herself to quell it immediately.

The pleasure had affected her, of course it had, but what she'd not expected was how emotionally penetrating the experience would be. How vulnerable and ridiculous it would leave her.

She had to tread carefully here. This man took lovers, he did not commit to them. He was dangerous and deviant and dreadfully unpredictable.

He'd leave her.

He'd take her, then he'd leave her.

Remember that, she told herself, even as she devoured the sight of him looming above her bed.

Silent as a reaper, and no less lethal.

His nostrils flared and his eyes gleamed. Breaths sawed in and out of him like the bellows of a furnace.

She was about to learn what it was to lie with a man.

Not to make love. He'd been very careful never to use those words.

To fuck.

That's what they were doing here.

He would teach her the delicate indignities of the carnal act. She would know why men used the words they did to describe the deed. Thrusting. Riding. Pounding. Claiming.

She would know the softness and the violence of it.

Wordlessly, his gaze seared down at her as his hands fell to the placket of his trousers, deftly undoing them and the garment beneath before letting it all fall from his lean hips.

Mercy stared at his naked form in breathless awe.

He was something more than gorgeous. A chiseled effigy of immaculate masculinity. Too perfect. Too large and vital for one woman.

He'd warned her.

True to form, she'd refused to listen.

And, as usual, she would have to reap the consequences.

One of which might be her very first broken heart.

CHAPTER 10

*R*aphael never sampled the substances his father—and now he—sold. Because he'd seen time and again what physical attachment did to a person.

How ruinous it became.

But as Mercy rose from the cobalt velvet swirls of her bed covers, like Calypso from the sea, he knew he was lost.

She might have been stripped to the skin, but she'd left him exposed and raw, down to the very essence of what made him a mortal.

A man.

Her flavor was ambrosia.

Her body an altar to the bacchanalian gods.

Her skin pale and soft or—in some places—peach and succulent.

That flesh called for him to reach for her now, but something in her eyes caused him to hesitate. A new expression she wore, both marvel and melancholy.

Withstanding her perusal was an exquisite torture.

But he'd been tortured before.

He'd survive it.

Better that she become used to the sight of him first,

117

to the idea of his body, before he fell upon her like the lustful beast tearing through his veins.

Though she seemed uncertain, she was the one to rise to her knees and reach out.

To close the gap between them.

Her questing hands branded fingertip-sized trails of fire over his shoulders, down his pectorals and across the ticklish spokes of his ribs.

He didn't dare move. Her innocent exploration of him was a most elegant agony, one he wasn't certain he ever wanted to escape.

She didn't take much time, impatient minx that she was. Didn't linger over his tattoos or his muscles, or the parts of him that were not foreign to her.

They both had arms, nipples, a stomach.

There was certainly a difference in shape between them, but not one that seemed to unduly concern her.

She looked him right in the eyes as slim, cool fingers wrapped around the girth of his throbbing sex, forcing a tight gasp from his constricting throat.

Heat collected behind his spine and pulled the pendulous weight beneath his cock tight into his body with the gathering spasms of release.

Groaning, he seized her hand.

"What's wrong?" she asked, eyes wide with concern. "Did I hurt you?"

He brought her knuckles to his mouth and kissed each precious one. "Quite the opposite. Your touch threatens to end this moment too quickly."

"I don't mind," she cajoled.

"*I* do." Affronted, he pulled her close for a searching kiss.

Didn't she understand that he needed this night to last forever?

Not only because he didn't have many nights left, but because even though he was a man who always claimed what he went after, he rarely went after what he truly wanted.

Somehow, this young, untried woman seemed to know what it was that he *needed*. Intrinsically answering questions he hadn't yet thought to ask.

Her fingers slid into his hair, both soothing him and setting the nerves there alight with sensation. He'd needed her touch, craved it, and yet a sense of guilt kept him from seeking it.

Tonight was his to give. To teach. To soothe and comfort. A woman's first time took patience and skill and reserve that only a knave would abandon.

His ferocious and terrible instinct would have him pin her to the bed while he remained standing so he could press her knees by her head and watch himself fuck and fuck and *fuck* her until they collapsed with thirst and exhaustion.

He wanted to feed her from his hand and bathe her so he could bend her over and do it again. He wanted her to tie him up and ride his mouth. His cock.

He wanted her in every depraved way a man could take a woman.

And the simple ones too...

Mercy Goode was inherently a carnal woman, given to impish mischief and endless curiosity. She wouldn't be content with basic, gentle lovemaking for long.

She'd want more.

And he'd be gone before long.

Holy Christ, she'd find someone else.

Possessive instinct surged, and suddenly she was in the circle of his arms, her lithe body clenched against his with such strength, he lifted her knees from the bed.

A turbulent rage rose beneath his lust, churning opaque emotions from where he'd forced them to lie dormant like the bed of sludge beneath a lake of ice.

Why now?

When decisions had been made, and his fate sealed. When he'd vowed to atone for all the wrong he'd never wanted to do...

The right woman barged into his life and turned his entire world upside down.

Made him question everything he thought he knew about himself.

Made him yearn for things that were patently impossible.

Made his blood froth and churn with torrents of need, and his heart trip and kick with boyish, frivolous emotions.

Like hope, for example.

Or whatever this odd amalgamation of impossible softness and desperate intensity could be called.

Was there a word for it?

For yearning more insatiable than lust? Hunger more excruciating than deprivation?

Pain more insidious than the shattering of bone?

The three languages he spoke fluently offered up nothing. Though, the feel of the naked woman molded to him might have addled his brain somewhat.

Her response to the imprisonment of his arms was unfettered and open and fearless, just like her.

Pressing herself to him, she scored his scalp with her nails, rolled her body in sinuous undulations, as if the entire ravenous intensification of their encounter had been *her* bloody idea.

In fact, she tugged at him with surprising strength for such a delicate creature, pulling him back to the bed and nearly climbing him like a falling tree as he lay her back on the counterpane.

Her thighs fell open beneath his weight, her long legs locking around his waist.

The delicate heat of her sex singed him with need.

"I'm ready," she sighed, her voice still husky from

her climax and her lashes fanning long shadows against her flushed cheek.

He bloody wasn't.

Or—rather—he *was*. Too ready. Too hungry. He wanted to shove into her like a brute. To rut like a stag and submit her like a stallion. If only he could crawl inside of her, somehow, to join with her in a way that would leave a part of him locked within her.

Christ, was this why people procreated?

Something about that thought sobered him a little. Enough to let him pull back and gaze down into her lovely face.

Her hair was a riot of precious metals in the lamplight. The strands at her nape a deep bronze, and those at her temple light as mercury. The tresses fanned out around her creamy shoulders in waves of corn silk and spun gold.

Eyes shining like brilliant sapphires, she flicked her little pink tongue across lips red and swollen from the abrasion of his kisses, as if savoring the taste of him there.

Or the flavor of her own desire.

The gesture nearly undid him.

Her pert nose flared with heavy gasps that fell against his face in sweet-scented puffs. Their shared breaths felt more intimate than the most immoral acts he'd ever committed.

Finally, he settled his hips into the cradle of hers, grunting as the crown of his cock slid against the wet cove of her body.

Her gaze showed no uncertainty and it lanced him all the way through. He'd done nothing in his entire benighted life to deserve such trust.

And yet. There it was.

"I'm sorry if I hurt you," he whispered, kissing her with a conciliatory tug of his lips.

"I forgive you," she whispered, squirming her hips in gasp-inducing impatience. "But only if you hurry."

If only all demands were so easy to satisfy.

If only all hurts were so easily forgiven.

Setting his jaw, Raphael nudged forward.

Initially her body gave, welcoming the plump crown of him with a slick kiss. When he encountered hindrance, he cursed viciously, stalling his progression.

"I'm sorry," she gasped, her features tight with concentration.

"No, *mon chaton*." He dropped kisses onto her cheekbones, her eyelids, the wisps of curls at her temples. "No. *I* am sorry. Tell me to stop." It would be a feat even Hercules might have failed, but he'd do it.

"You're trembling," she remarked, smoothing her palms over his shoulders shaking with the burden of his restraint.

"I—I can't bring myself to hurt you."

"I'm not in pain. Just...pressure." She wriggled against him again, testing the barrier.

Jesus. Fuck.

He couldn't do this. Not with her. Not *to* her.

When he made to withdraw, she gripped at him with sharp claws, her nails creating delicious little crescents of pain on his back.

"Do it," she commanded, her features becoming a mask of determination before she buried her face against his neck. "Do it. Now."

He could do nothing but obey.

With a surge of his hips, he impaled her.

Her teeth sank into the meat of his shoulder and she gave a whimper that gutted him.

Gathering her close, he curled around her as they each shuddered and surrendered to the feel of him seated inside to the hilt.

Their breaths synchronized, as the tight clutch of

her molded around him. Eventually the pulsing muscles milked at his cock, seeming to pull him even deeper, like a fist of wet silk.

He could come like this. Deep inside of her. Without moving anything.

The Fauve that he was desired just that. He could simply bathe her womb in his seed, thinking it could take root.

How could it not when he was so deliciously deep?

Never. An insidious inner voice reminded him. You promised to *never.*

A hasty breath created a movement where they were joined. And the noise she made stirred him.

A sigh of curious delight.

Encouraged, he rolled his hips slightly and she responded each time with tiny sounds in her throat. Little mewls, like that a kitten would make.

His kitten.

Mon chaton.

Then she said the most dangerous words one could utter to a man like him.

"More. I want more."

It was all he needed.

He gave it to her, in long, deliberate—if careful—thrusts. He fed her his length once. And again. And again. Wedging himself impossibly deeper each time.

Her arms clutched at him, her lush mouth opening in a silent quest for a kiss, but he denied her.

He had to watch, to see the play of emotion run across her face. To observe what he wrought inside of her. The astonishment and the acceptance. The heat and the hunger. The shuddering surrender.

Raphael knew the moment she'd become a prisoner to her pleasure. It pulled her away from him. Unfocused her eyes and brought her entire concentration inward. He knew what his languorous strokes built, that the angle of their hips created friction not only inside but against the engorged knot of sensation that was the button to every woman's desire.

Sweat bloomed between them, creating a damp, erotic slide of flesh against flesh. It was as if they had fused into one, that he'd become buried so deep inside her body, that he might have reason to hope to lodge himself in her heart, as well.

Their limbs tangled in untidy knots, mirroring his emotions.

Perhaps if he entwined them so thoroughly, there would be no unraveling them.

This.

This was the danger of addiction.

When something took you away from yourself. When it became as essential as air or water. Oblivion merged into sensation and colors fused into high-relief and time lost all meaning. Perhaps the future was a memory. Or the past was a lie.

Or there was only this.

This moment. This joy. This act. This emotion.

This woman.

He'd not expected her to come again. Not her first time.

But when her spine arched and her sex spasmed around him in delicious contractions, something like panic surged as his own climax gathered through his veins.

It sped toward him, an avalanche bent on annihilation. He already knew how powerful it would be and still couldn't leap out of the way.

It would ruin him. Shatter him.

He barely pulled out in time.

Burying a roar in the velvet of her quilt, he let his cock slide between their bodies as his release ripped him apart. It was a cataclysm of pleasure, something so mind-altering he knew the moment defined him.

Because there was the resolute man he'd been before he tasted the heaven that was the embrace of Mercy Goode.

And the tragedy of everything that was about to happen next.

CHAPTER 11

*M*ercy thought that relinquishing her virginity would make her feel older, somehow. More experienced and womanly. Perhaps even wise, now that she'd been initiated into the society of secret smiles shared by Nora and Pru, her two married sisters.

Instead, she felt very young and vulnerable as she complacently allowed Raphael to wipe away the slick leavings of their joining from her belly and between her thighs.

She stared at the shoes he'd discarded in haste. The one's he'd wear to leave her.

Would he put them on? Was it time for him to go now?

Now that she was cold and oddly small and lonely in her massive bed.

Mercy took a moment to admire the masculine shape of his backside as he turned away from her and ministered to his own hygiene.

She wished she were a sculptor. A painter. Any sort of artist that could capture him in a rendering.

For memories had a tendency to fade, and she wanted to appreciate his beauty every day.

He returned to her, and her heart lifted as he slid into the bed and gathered her against him. Settling on his back, he arranged her boneless limbs over his muscled form like a marionette before spreading her curls across his chest so he could stroke her hair with lazy fingers.

She nuzzled into him as he yawned with such ferocity his jaw cracked and his limbs shuddered with it.

As elegant and sinister as he was with his fine suits and caustic conversation, Mercy discovered she rather liked him like this.

Silky hair mussed by her fingers in the throes of pleasure, hazel eyes at half-mast and a drowsy curve softening his hard mouth. Even his jaw had relaxed, the cords beneath his ears and next to his temple released.

The damp chill of the late-winter night lurked just outside of where their cobalt coverlet and gold lamp ensconced them in a decadence of warmth and flesh and velvet.

Though he'd pulled the blanket to their waists, she could still consider their differences with idle curiosity. Decide what she liked and what she had to accustom herself to...

If that were an option.

The steely muscle beneath his marble-smooth skin mesmerized her as she let her fingers wander the peaks and valleys of his geography. She appreciated all that he was, the dusky hue to his skin. The warm fragrance of him, like cotton and salt.

Crisp hair on his leg tickled the inside of her thigh, and she drew her appendage over the abrading stuff, letting it scratch away the irksome itch.

His breath evened. Moving from the chest beneath her cheek down to his stomach. The hammer of his heart slowed to a thump, and he was silent for so long she thought he might have fallen asleep.

She lifted her head to check and found him staring —unblinking—into the middle distance as his fingers toyed with her hair.

"Is something troubling you?" she asked, pretending not to be anxious as she perched her head on her palm.

He was not quick to reply. "I don't know if it's the darkness of the hour or of the situation, but I can only think it is a cruelty of fate that I found you."

"Well...there's a thing to say." A frown tugged at her mouth, at her heart, and she pushed back from him, offended in the extreme. "When I was feeling just the opposite. Thinking how fortunate I was to have spent such a time with you. To have enjoyed myself so thoroughly. Did I..um... Have I misunderstood your seemingly enthusiastic responses?"

"No, no, sweet Mercy, that is not what I meant." He cupped her chin, cradling it as if it were made of spun glass. "It is cruel to have a night like this, knowing I cannot have another. It tinged this incomparable pleasure with exquisite pain."

"We *could* do it again." She brightened, his words a balm for her bruised heart, even as she lamented the idea of losing him. "My parents have extended their stay on the continent another month. And even after they arrive home, I could finagle a way to occasionally meet you at the Savoy or—"

He shook his head, his eyes abysmal wells of bleak despair. "*Mon coeur*, you mustn't care for me. You mustn't become attached."

Mon coeur. My heart. How could he call her something like that and then insist there was nothing further between them?

Was the endearment just a sweet and flippant nothing to him?

She cocked her head. "Do you care for nothing? For no one?"

He drew in a long breath through his nose. "It has been my secret all these years. I have gained so much because I didn't care if I lost it. I risk everything when I take a gamble, and I have not lost for so long...until now."

"What do you mean?"

He speared her with a gaze so intense she felt as if it punctured her all the way through. "I told you I only love one person on this earth, and I referred to Gabriel, but...I am in danger of falling for you, Mercy Goode."

She blinked at the immediacy of his confession. He hadn't said love, though the word lingered on the periphery of their conversation. "I've heard it said that men in bed are often men in love. You do not know me enough to fall—"

He coiled at the waist, levering to a sitting position so as to bracket her cheeks with his hands, capturing her face in a gentle prison so he might bore the truth of his words into her. "I want you to know that I have been unable to stop thinking about you since the moment we met. That is something—"

"Yes," she clipped. "That is something I've heard before. Is it not easier to imagine that you are infatuated with my youth and beauty than with me?"

"I cannot contest that you are the loveliest creature, but your sister is equally handsome and stirs me not at all. It is not only this chemistry between us that draws me to you. It is everything. Your entire bold, adventurous, domineering, warrior's spirit. It is the life that spills from you, that radiates like a star in the middle of your own solar system. You don't just tempt me, you *fascinate* me—obsess me—and no one has managed to do that in a very long time."

"Then..." She cast her gaze down and schooled the longing from her voice. "Why not continue this while we are inclined to do so?"

"Because the moment I care for something...someone...it gives them power over me."

"Your enemies?"

"Yes, but I was referring to...my men."

At that, she sat up straighter, folding her legs beneath the sheets to face him fully. "I don't understand."

His face softened and his gaze touched every part of her face, as if committing it to memory. "That is because you are not part of this brutal world in which I exist, and I would not have it touch you. I will—die first."

Mercy's brows crimped as she did her utmost to puzzle him out. One thing missing from the mysteries of Eddard Sharpe was this vagary of fate. The villains were dastardly characters motivated by hatred, greed, or any number of ugly impulses belonging to man.

Rarely—never—were they noble or tender with predispositions toward generosity and kindness.

This man, this wicked, rakish criminal was possessed of a conscience. A code.

And yet...

"Why did you become a Fauve?" she asked, knowing she tread on dangerous ground. "Furthermore, why lead them if they would so easily turn on you? What sort of life is that?"

"It's the life Gabriel and I inherited," he answered simply, as if he'd resigned himself to such a disappointment long ago.

"Inherited?" she echoed.

"From *le Bourreau*." He muttered the name as if it tasted of ashes in his mouth. "The Executioner."

He slumped against her headboard, the covers sliding around his lean waist. Broad shoulders rolled forward a little as if Atlas himself could not have contained such a burden. His eyes unfocused slightly, as he looked into the past.

• • •

"HE WAS an Englishman who married a Monégasque girl—my mother—leveraged by the debts her father owed him," he explained in a voice devoid of emotion. "He kept her—us—in a villa in Monaco where he ruled the underworld there. Gaming establishments, brothels, and smuggling ships..." His fists curled in her bedclothes as his eyes glittered with a hatred so cold and absolute, she shivered with it.

"Fighting rings."

Mercy covered his taut fist with her hand, and it unclenched beneath the pressure until he turned it to thread his fingers with hers.

"Your father, he...died?" she asked gently.

His jaw worked to the side in a show of gall. "My mother went first, suffered terribly from the syphilis he gave her, and he lingered—too long—disintegrating until parts of his body rotted away, to match the soul beneath."

Mercy hadn't been faced with such animosity before, not really. Her relationship with her father was either cold or contentious, but all they felt for each other was a rather mild form of duty and disappointment.

Raphael hated his father with a rage-induced loathing she'd not known him capable of.

It frightened her.

"Did he...was he...awful to you?" she queried.

His expression was carefully impassive. "He was horrible to everyone. I was no exception."

"You should have been." Mercy ventured closer to him, wanting to provide him comfort but feeling ill-equipped to do so. "You were his son."

"His second son."

"Did you resent that?"

"Never," he answered darkly. "I was glad to be a small, rather undeveloped boy even after fourteen or so. I was lucky that he ignored me. That he thought me too pathetic to much notice."

"Why would you be glad of that?" she asked, thinking she already knew she didn't want the answer.

"Gabriel was always so extraordinarily big and strong and as savage as my father had crafted him to be. He was heir apparent to the Lord of Louts. And the prince to those who called themselves the Fauves. And still, when my father needed money, he threw Gabriel to the pits."

"Is...that why he wears a mask?"

Raphael nodded, swallowing once. Twice.

"My brother always protected me from my father and now, you understand, it is my job to protect him."

"I understand," she murmured. And she did. It never mattered what kind of man he'd wanted to be. Because he was who his father made him. "So, like the monarchy, when the king of the Fauves dies, his sons inherit?"

"Only if they are worthy. If they can command the respect of the men."

"What if you didn't want to be a part of it anymore? What if you gave the mantle over to another?"

He dragged a finger over her cheek, his gaze gentle and resigned. "Would that I could, *mon chaton*, but men in our world can only escape by dying. There are too many secrets between us, too much at stake. These men are often criminals because they have no one to trust, nowhere to turn for protection from poverty and despair. That sort of desperation turns a man into a beast. Men like my father turn those beasts into soldiers. Gives them a code. A family to die for. To kill for. A way to advance. And, like in the wilds, the pack will turn upon you if you show weakness. If they can no longer rely upon you to provide."

To be held captive by power, she could barely imagine it. "So...if you were not born into this life, you would not have chosen it?"

"Never."

"What would you have done instead?"

"I would have been a ship's captain," he answered without thought.

"Oh?"

He glanced at her astonished expression with a wry twist of his lips. "It's the only part of my position I truly enjoy. When we transport overseas, I've taken to the mechanics and running of the ship itself...not that it matters now."

"Of course, it matters." She squeezed his hand. "It's significant to me."

He snorted. "Why? Because you can now imagine a different reality in which I am a good man?"

"You laugh, but I'm not entirely convinced you're a bad one."

A rueful sound escaped him as he drew a knuckle down the curve of her shoulder, following it all the way to her elbow. "Believe me, I am."

"Well, ironically enough, I'm not a good girl, either."

That cleared some of the ice from his gaze. "Yes, you are."

"Shows what you know!" she said. "I'm forever disappointing everyone. Making mischief, saying the wrong things, wanting what I ought not to...fighting to change the world."

"Please don't ever stop," he whispered, his fingers digging into her waist to nudge her closer. "Instead, change the world to suit you, Mercy Goode; if anyone could, it'd be you." He lowered his head to nudge at her nose with his own. "I—I only wish I could be here to see it."

She blinked. "Tell me where you are going."

"Nowhere." He tossed her a charming, brilliant smile and seized her, rolling them over until she was straddling his torso with her hands braced over his glorious chest. "At least not tonight."

CHAPTER 12

Raphael just paid an enormous fortune for a lie.

But no world existed where Gabriel would allow for his real plans to come to fruition, so he kept up pretenses for his brother's sake.

The man in question studied his identification papers with precise and methodical sweeps of his eyes, as if committing even the fine print to memory.

"When I wake, I'll be Gareth Severand." Gabriel tested the words in his graveled voice and winced as if they tasted strange in his mouth.

Dr. Titus Conleith leaned a hip against his desk where they'd gathered in his hospital office. "I was told by Frank Walters—who sends his regards along with your new identities—that keeping names somewhat similar in cadence and lettering helps one assimilate and identify easier."

While Gabriel folded his limbs into one of the chairs across from the desk, Raphael turned to pacing. The room was as warm and masculine as its master. The overstuffed furniture and landscape canvasses seemed incongruous with the sterile environs of the rest of the hospital.

This was where Conleith took people to tell them that they or their loved ones were going to die, Raphael suspected.

And in a way, that's exactly what he was telling them now.

Gabriel and Raphael Sauvageau would be essentially deceased after tonight.

Once Gabriel went under the knife, Raphael was supposed to set a plan in motion to implode the Fauves from the inside.

"You've barely glanced at your papers, Rafe," Gabriel prompted, lifting his chin to peek over at his identification.

Raphael screwed on a sardonic smile. "That's Remy Severand to you."

Titus studied them from beneath his somber brow, his sharp bronze eyes always seeming to conduct an examination, even when one wasn't his patient. "Have you decided where you're going to land when this is all said and done?" he asked. "Not Monaco, surely."

"Too much past there to have a future." Gabriel shook his head adamantly, adjusting his mask as if eager to be rid of the thing. "Perhaps someday we'll return to Normandy or France, but I think for the time being, we'll lose ourselves in the West.

Raphael nodded in agreement.

Titus bucked his hip away from his desk and reached for the white coat draped over his elegant chair. "I think it's marvelous you get a fresh start away from your tainted legacy. I'm a firm believer in second chances." He punched his arms into the coat and reached the door in a few long-legged strides. "I'm going to go make certain the surgical theater is prepared. I'll leave you two to say your goodbyes before the procedure. It'll be...lengthy."

Say your goodbyes. The doctor had no idea how final that sounded.

Because it was.

Raphael didn't want to say goodbye. He hated them.

It was why—even though every fiber that stitched his body together had felt adhered to the heaven that was Mercy Goode's bed—he'd peeled himself away to vanish before dawn illuminated her cherubic face.

Because he might have given in to the insatiable urge to have her once more.

Or the impossible desire to stay.

As Gabriel took another moment to study the papers in his hands, Raphael studied him.

He'd a patchwork body, that was for certain. His ruined face wasn't the only place he carried scars. His arms and chest had become a canvass of tattoos decorating a physique that was a monument to power.

And to violence.

But nothing felled his brother.

Nothing.

That wasn't about to change. Gabriel had survived so many things that would have crushed most other men.

He'd likewise survive Raphael's loss. He would keep his word and go to America to spread Mathilde's ashes.

Then, he'd live the life they both craved.

The one Gabriel deserved.

"I'd like a final smoke before I go under the knife." Gabriel stood, reaching into his jacket pocket.

It occurred to Raphael, not for the first time, that his brother looked almost amusingly incongruous in such finery. His neck didn't like a collar and his jaw always wanted shaving, even after a razor had been taken to it. Though his mask was meticulously crafted, it made for a sinister, unsightly spectacle.

Better that than the terror beneath.

Raphael followed his brother outside, watching Gabriel's ritual of pulling the hood low against any kind of weather for the last time. When he woke—when he healed—he'd have a face he could show to the world.

Raphael wished he'd be able to see it.

Gabriel rested his shoulders against the grey stone of the hospital, bending his knee to prop the sole of his boot on the wall. A passerby might imagine that the towering man held up the building, rather than the other way around.

This was harder than Raphael had expected. He wanted to stay. He wanted to run. He wanted for the thousandth time...a life that hadn't been fucked before he was even born. "Do you want me to stay until you're asleep?" He asked the question with a demonstrative fondness he wasn't prone to.

If Gabriel noticed, he didn't say. "Nah. You've work to do." He poked the tamper into the bowl of his pipe. The instrument looked comically tiny in his hands, something like a child's toy. "Besides, that was always my responsibility."

Their gazes locked.

Yes, Gabriel had always stood watch over him. Had taken the wrath of their father upon his gigantic shoulders. When they were boys, Raphael's nightmares would plague him, and Gabriel would sit up with him, both a sentinel against and savior from the nightmares in the dark.

The day he'd become so disfigured, it had been Raphael's turn in the pits. He'd been so young and scrawny.

Terrified.

Gabriel had shoved him in a locker and taken his place in the ring.

This was why Raphael would die for him...

"Have you ever thought what we'll do...after this?" Gabriel's pensive question interrupted his reverie.

Raphael blinked against the drizzle and a little confusion. "Do?"

Gabriel made an impatient gesture. "You know, in America, or wherever we settle. What will we *do* with ourselves?" He struck a match against the rough edge of the stone and cupped his hand over the flame as he touched it to the fragrant tobacco in his pipe.

"Live like kings, that's what you'll do. There's fortune enough that your children's children's children won't have to worry. You'll do whatever you bloody well please."

Gabriel sank deeper into his hood as Honoria Goode dashed by, one arm shielding her lovely hat with a newspaper, and the other hand lifting her skirts as she nearly skipped up the stairs to the hospital to avoid the rain.

Even she didn't know what her husband was about to do. Conleith had agreed it was safer.

Raphael's eyes followed Mercy's eldest sister, his eyes hungry for any sort of reminder of her. She and Honoria were as different in coloring as night was from day. The elder two Goode sisters had midnight hair and large dark eyes, but her jaw was crafted with the same sharp lines and stubborn angles. Her shape formed with the same delicate perfection.

Raphael licked his lips, thinking he could still find hints of Mercy's incomparable flavor on them.

"Children..." Gabriel exhaled the word on a long puff of smoke. "I've never allowed myself to think of something like that. Even if I'd ever been able to convince a woman to— Well, I'd never thought to maintain our legacy. I suppose I'd hoped our father's seed would die with us, perhaps his violence would, too."

Raphael feigned his usual irreverent mirth. "Likely not, I've probably got a million bastards out running around somewhere. Find you a handsome hazel-eyed tramp and I've probably boffed his mother."

"I know you better." Gabriel's solemnity wiped the smile from Raphael's face.

Because he was right.

Raphael was as careful as he could be, even in his conquests. He'd never wanted to sire a child, to assign the poor thing a bastard's status.

A bastard that would have become an orphan.

He'd always known he'd make a shit father.

"Why are you asking about the future, anyhow?" he clipped, stealing the pipe from his brother and taking an uncharacteristically long inhale.

He'd never been much of a smoker, but it certainly couldn't hurt to start on today of all days.

His last day.

"Couldn't tell you." Gabriel scanned the bustle of the streets. Streets they'd claimed to own, corners upon which they'd done business for ages. "Who am I, if not a fighter? Who are we, if not criminals, thieves, and smugglers? I'm going to wake up with this name, Gareth, and it tastes wrong in my mouth. Maybe it wouldn't...if I had a purpose."

"Well, you'll have a few bloody weeks to brood on it in the hospital while your face is gooping back together...I wouldn't worry about it. Things won't change so much."

Gabriel retrieved the pipe from him and took another draw. "You don't know that."

"I know you'll have all this gold to spend, and don't worry, I'm pretty sure you'll still be dog-fuckingly ugly, so that will at least be familiar." Raphael punched him in the shoulder.

Usually, a bit of banter cheered his brother, but not today. "The doctor said there would still be scars."

"Sure, but you'll have a fucking nose, won't you? Besides." He waggled dark brows. "Posh birds who crave a bit of rough will ask to kiss your scars, see if they don't."

Gabriel shook his head and shoved him back. "Get on with you, now."

Raphael knew his brother couldn't smile. The scars wouldn't allow it. But he remembered what Gabriel's mirth looked like.

And that was enough. He superimposed the memory over what was left of his brother's face.

Inside, he felt exactly how Gabriel looked. Destroyed by lashes, slashes...

And scars.

"Gabriel, if anything should happen—that is—if it takes me too long to get to the Indies, go to America without me. I'm having Mathilde's ashes sent to—"

Gabriel perked at that. "You're leaving almost a month ahead of me, of course you'll get there first."

"Of course, but you never know...plans go awry."

Pushing himself off the wall, Gabriel towered over him, staring down hard from his one good eye. "Are you thinking of staying for *her*? Because it's not possible. It's too dangerous for them both."

"I don't know what you're talking about." Raphael had to turn away. What a shit time to realize he was terrible at lying to his brother.

He wasn't going to stay.

He was going where no one could follow. Going to find his father in hell and be part of the bevy of demons tormenting the bastard for eternity.

"I saw you last night." Gabriel's low murmur whipped his head around.

"Pardon?"

"Sneaking into Cresthaven." His brother picked a sliver of tobacco from his tongue.

"Are you following me?"

"No."

Raphael narrowed one eye at him. "Then what were *you* doing at Cresthaven?"

It was Gabriel's turn to look away. "I had business nearby."

"No, you bloody didn't."

"It doesn't matter." Gabriel made a dismissive gesture. "It said on the police records that Felicity Goode was in the police wagon with you, but that wasn't her. It was her twin."

Raphael didn't have to feign indignance this time. "How can you tell them apart? You've spent all of five seconds in their company."

"Felicity doesn't speak like Mercy." Gabriel's voice changed in a way that sparked a dark and painful knowledge in Raphael's gut. There was a reverence there. Something that echoed in his own hollowed-out soul. "She doesn't move so sharply through the world. So decisively. Her steps are...careful. Her words are soft."

Raphael narrowed his eyes at his brother. It couldn't be... "You were at Cresthaven last night watching Felicity Goode? For *shame*, you voyeur!" He nudged at him with an elbow.

"I *am* ashamed." Gabriel refused to be mollified. "I can't help but wonder if I feature in any of her nightmares."

"I'm certain she's forgotten you even exist," Raphael said over a derisive noise.

That didn't seem to make it better.

"This isn't...guilt, is it, brother?" he accused. "You like her. You *want* her."

Gabriel had looked at women before, but he'd never watched them. Not like this. He seemed to have come to terms early in life with the fact that his face condemned him to the life of a monk.

"Two brothers tempted by two sisters." Gabriel made a grunt that might have been humor or grief. "It's all rather Shakespearean, isn't it? One of the tragedies, in our case."

"I'd never love Mercy Goode," Raphael claimed, wondering why he still felt as though he were lying to his brother. "It wouldn't be safe for her. But...I didn't want to leave without..." He couldn't seem to finish his sentence.

"You're not being cruel to her, are you? Didn't leave her with promises that will break her heart?"

That Gabriel even cared surprised him more than he could express.

Ultimately, he shook his head. "No. She is in no need of entanglements. That woman has made it abundantly clear, a man would only get in her way."

Gabriel nodded, taking a deep breath of the crisp air, turning his face to the sky to let the rain plink against his mask.

"Don't worry about Mercy and Felicity Goode," Raphael advised, though whether to Gabriel or himself, he couldn't quite figure. "They have a fierce bond, unshakable trust, and a future together."

"As do we, *brother*. As do we." Gabriel turned to him and clasped his shoulder in a rare show of fraternal affection. "Enjoy your last few weeks as the handsome one, Rafe. Or should I say, Remy? I'll see you in Antigua."

Raphael could only bring himself to nod.

Turning, Gabriel conquered the steps to the grand building with an almost jubilant jog, taking two at a time.

The next words were lost to the soft sound of the rain as it pattered against the cobbles of the streets that would become his grave.

"Goodbye, *mon frere. Vive la vie.*"

Live life.

CHAPTER 13

*M*ercy resolutely *did not* think of Raphael all the next day.

She awoke to find he'd vanished like the night mist off the Thames when the sun burned it away. If not for the whisper of heat and the musk of his aftershave haunting his side of the bed, one might have thought last night nothing but a fever dream.

She rolled over and buried her face in the pillow he'd so unceremoniously abandoned. Intimate muscles ached and protested in a way that was both wicked and dispiriting.

He was gone.

Of course, he would be. She'd expected it. Accepted it. And refused to feel any sort of ridiculous melancholy about it.

Except...had he even kissed her goodbye? Did she sleep through it?

Or had he simply slithered away like a wary thief in the shadows, grateful to be spared any inconvenient or emotional farewells?

Not that he'd have had to suffer such nonsense.

They'd both understood that they were lovers for one night only.

And, Holy Moses, did they ever make the most of their evening.

She'd had him three times in three different ways, though he'd sent her rocketing into the stars a total of five.

Dear God, but was he insatiable. She'd had to beg for respite, and only *then* did he wrap his large, warm body around her and lull her to sleep with his even breaths stirring her hair.

She refused to be sentimental about it, dammit. She wasn't one of those ridiculous women who took to their beds when neglected by a man.

It was only that...she'd felt like a treasure lying wrapped in his embrace. Something coveted and rare.

It'd been rather lovely.

Different.

It wasn't that she *needed* to feel that way, of course. She'd come to terms with the fact that she was a thorn in the collective side of the world at large.

Forever too much or not enough.

It was just that, the sensation of fitting so perfectly against his hips, her head resting in the deep groove of his chest. The way the tempo of their hearts seemed to harmonize with the effortless synchronization of their breath.

For the moment in between waking and the oblivion of sleep, she'd felt like a part of him.

Rather than *apart* from the world.

Perhaps because she was untried in the ways of intimacy. Affection wasn't something their family encouraged. Or even condoned.

That had to be it.

Raphael's disappearance wasn't the architect of this strange sense of attachment and loss. This empty sort of yearning that hollowed out the space behind her breast.

It was simply that she was untried and unaccustomed to such an arrangement, and needed to amend her reaction to it, lest she become some simpering ninny and do something atrocious.

Like cry over Raphael Sauvageau.

How many tears had fallen for the rake? Likely enough to fill the Atlantic.

Hers would *not* be added to the tide.

She had work to do. A murderer to find. And no mere man would get in the way of her mission. All she had to do was be unwavering in her relinquishment of him. Not allow him to permeate her other incredibly weighty thoughts and important tasks.

He would, no doubt, attend the masquerade that evening, but it was best she avoid him as he'd made it clear in no uncertain terms that he didn't want her there.

Well...she wasn't one to be ordered about.

She would take a weapon. Would stay in safe and crowded areas with plenty of witnesses.

And she'd solve the murder before him, by Jove.

See if she didn't.

That decided, she did a marvelous job of *not* thinking about him all day.

She didn't think of him as she lingered over breakfast and read the newspapers in bed. Because such an activity would surely *not* be enjoyable with a companion. It wouldn't do to imagine all sorts of amusing opinions he might have about things. Or wonder if he'd maybe share a nibble of her toast. A man his size probably had quite the appetite of a morning...

Did he prefer tea or coffee?

It didn't matter, she forcefully reminded herself. It didn't bear consideration.

She *did not* think of him when she soaked in the

bath and scrubbed the memory of his clever—no, *masterful*—fingers and mouth from her skin.

He'd been inside of her. Joined with her.

What a novel thing that a human could connect with another in such a way...that they were made to do just this. To delight in it.

Did everyone fit together so perfectly? Was their pleasure so overcoming and instinctual?

She wanted to find out, but something told her that to do so with another man would find her disappointed.

Better not to wonder. Not to dwell.

Did he feel altered somehow by their night together? Like it merited some sort of distinction. Like a change in the very map of the stars?

Why would he? Why would anyone?

She *did not* think of him when she viciously chopped the heads off their hothouse flowers for her maid to arrange in her hair.

Nor when she selected a dagger to strap to her leg.

She wasn't angry. She wasn't hurt.

She didn't miss him.

She didn't even *know* him.

Unlike Detective Eddard Sharpe, Mercy had not mastered the art of infiltration and disguise.

Not yet, in any case.

So, she was incandescently glad when Felicity insisted upon accompanying her to the Midwinter Masquerade. Social functions were not her sister's forte, as such, but Felicity's attachment and sense of obligation to Mathilde's memory was no less intense than her own.

They dressed in identical sapphire gowns and donned masks the color of the moon on an overcast evening, intricately decorated with gems and filigree.

Once again forgoing her spectacles proved to make the night interesting for Felicity.

Mercy might have told her sister about her night with Raphael, if she'd been allowing herself to think of it.

But she wasn't.

~

MERCY REMEMBERED her father once reading from the Bible about a den of iniquity. The phrase haunted her now as she watched the spectacle that was the Midwinter Masquerade. It made the sedate balls she attended appear like absolute child's play.

Killgore Keep was a grand old Plantagenet fortress that'd been renovated over the years by obscenely wealthy owners. It hunkered next to a quaint canal complete with a Tudor-era mill and extensive grounds. Amelia Trent, the widow of Captain Rupert Trent, a long-dead hero of the now defunct East India Company, was the first woman to own the keep. She spent her late husband's ill-begotten fortune as a patroness for artists of all kinds, and a rumored haven for the darker, more deviant side of the bohemian set. Mrs. Trent was famous for her bacchanalian fêtes, and her February spectacle was said to be a bombastic balm for the late-winter gloom.

Mathilde had procured Mercy an invitation, as they were to abscond that very evening.

Mercy made certain to impress herself upon the footman as she arrived so that when Felicity followed a quarter hour after, he'd assume he was merely allowing her reentry.

The ruse worked splendidly, and after she and her sister met for a moment in an alcove to work their stratagem, they broke apart, doing their best not to be seen together.

In such a massive manse, stuffed to the brim with the celebrities of the *demimonde*, it wasn't difficult to remain obscure.

Not only did they need to find the Duchesse de la Cour, they also endeavored to ascertain if there was a chance Gregoire had found out about Mathilde's lover. The Archambeaus' innermost circle of friends might have known about Mathilde's infidelity, and Mercy had a list of names to approach. Even though Gregoire himself had left the country, there was a possibility he'd found the money to pay for his wife's demise.

After an hour or so of idle but probing conversation —and not so idle eavesdropping—Mercy found herself both perplexed and concerned. There were not merely artists, actresses, naughty nobles in attendance, but a rather disproportionate congregation of rough-looking and incongruously well-dressed men.

Some were part of the joviality, drinking and dancing beneath the massive crystal chandeliers, or playing chance in one of the many illegal game rooms. Others tucked themselves in corners or alcoves, locked in conversations.

Or illicit embraces.

People sniffed powders from snuff boxes and smoked pungent substances from hookahs, pipes, and elegant cigarette holders.

Mercy was aware of an expectancy hovering over the gathering.

As if something violent waltzed in their midst, waiting for the right moment to unleash unholy chaos. She thought it must be why people celebrated and laughed uncommonly loud, in an attempt to drown out the low din of their disquiet.

Did they not see certain men placed strategically

around the manse? Adjacent to the revelry but taking no part of it.

Like sentinels.

Waiting.

Were these men all Fauves, perhaps? If so...how did they gain entry?

And where was their leader?

Mercy lurked just out of sight of the ballroom where she peeked in to find that Felicity had been escorted to the dance floor and might have been floating on a cloud in the arms of an elegant man with a roguish mask.

Her sister was not the easiest of conversationalists, but she'd always been an extraordinary dancer. Fluid and graceful and astonishingly comfortable.

It was the only time she forgot to be afraid, Mercy supposed. The music would sweep her away, and she knew the steps so well, her perfection was artless. She didn't have to look at her partner, nor did she have to talk to them if she didn't want to.

She positively glowed, and Mercy wasn't the only person to appreciate that.

Her sister really failed to notice how often men stared at her.

Or maybe she did realize, and that's what made her so afraid all the time.

Too often, the notice of a man was a dangerous thing.

One figure in particular stood half in the shadow of the grand staircase, his features shrouded by a lupine mask. Something in the way he stood, so absolutely still surrounded by chaos.

Like a mountain besieged by storms.

"Your sister is a beautiful dancer."

Goosebumps erupted all over Mercy's body at the

seductive murmur, tinged with a French accent, that slid like a blade into her ear.

Partly because she'd been so intent on the shade of the wolf, it distressed her that someone could have crept so close. And partly, because she'd not heard that sort of sensual appreciation in the voice of a *woman*.

Whirling, she found herself staring into the gentle leonine eyes of a statuesque lady with a wealth of russet hair. She'd the regal bearing of a queen, though the elegant hands in her crimson gloves trembled slightly.

"I did not think you would come. Not after Mathilde—" She broke off, swallowing twice before continuing. "I suppose I must introduce myself. My name is Amelie Beauchamp, Duchesse de la Cour. Which one the Misses Goode are you? The kind-hearted Felicity, or the delightful Mercy?"

"I can't speak to delightful, but I am Mercy Goode." Bewildered, she took the woman's extended hand and gave the ghost of a curtsy. For a villainess, the Duchesse certainly did have a dulcet voice. One only made for gentle solariums and sedate rose gardens, not such turmoil as this.

"I have heard you are asking after Mathilde tonight." The Duchesse watched her carefully from behind a mask the color of burgundy wine and gold. "Am I to presume that you are searching for the architect of her demise?"

"Her *murderer*, yes." Even though the woman apparently kept a tight rein on her composure, she thought she saw a reaction to the word.

Not a flinch, per se. But something close to it.

As the waltz ended, the two women took a moment to study each other while the shift in dance partners caused a din above which it was difficult to converse.

The Duchesse de la Cour was an incredibly elegant figure. Though uncommonly tall, her undeniable presence had less to do with her stature than the fine set of her jaw, the fullness of her lips, the sense of both wisdom and fragility emanating from her.

Could this woman bedecked in rubies and silk and swathed in an atmosphere of gracious courtesy be capable of murder?

Mercy didn't have to look to see that her sister had appeared at her elbow. She could always tell when Felicity was near with a satisfying sort of click, like that when a puzzle piece found its place.

One could only call the Duchesse's smile fond as she welcomed Felicity into their midst. "In her letters to me, Mathilde did not exaggerate your uncommon resemblance. I feel as if I know you two merely from your antics."

"Letters?" Taken aback, Mercy said the word with more emphasis than it called for. "I was under the impression Mathilde came here to *escape* you. Or at least the scandal you caused."

The Duchesse gave their surroundings a furtive glance. She gestured to a cozy cluster of furniture arranged in a shadowed corner by a billiard table that had evidently been abandoned in the middle of a game.

They drifted to it, the Duchesse sweeping a glass of champagne from a passing footman on her way.

Mercy sat with her back to the corner, noting the Duchesse did the same.

She wasn't certain who the other woman was keeping an eye out for, but in Mercy's case, it was certainly *not* Raphael.

Not in the least.

"Tell me, Your Grace, have you come to collect whatever it was Mathilde allegedly stole from you?" she asked, spearing the woman with a look she imagined an inquisitor might employ.

"*Mercy,*" Felicity admonished in a whisper as she settled herself across from them on a high-backed chair. "Perhaps we shouldn't be antagonistic just now."

"It's all right." The Duchesse tipped her glass of wine back and drained half of it in two bracing swallows. After taking a moment to compose herself, she said, "There *was* a scandal with Mathilde and me...and it had to do with treasure, but not jewels or trinkets. Something infinitely more priceless." She cast Mercy a meaningful look. "Is it not said that the heart is worth more than any fortune?"

"Love?" Mercy's eyes peeled wide with sudden comprehension at the same time her sister gasped.

She regarded the Duchesse, recalling what Mathilde had said about her lover. Dark. Handsome. Mysterious. Foreign. Sensual...

The woman was all of these things.

Long lashes swept down behind her mask. "I am sorry if I have shocked you, I almost thought Mathilde might have confided in you about me, as you were to bring her to me. I can't imagine what you must be thinking." The Duchesse finished her wine with a morose sigh.

"I'm thinking you were both going to leave your husbands and run away together."

"You would be right," she nodded. "The ship you were going to conduct her to belongs to me. I am the Duc de la Cour's second wife, and he has taken to his deathbed, as they say. I can't think that it's soon enough." Her bitterness was not at all concealed by her mask.

"My stepson, Armand, has made my life untenable, and so I have taken the money that is mine and had arranged for Mathilde and me to sail to foreign ports indefinitely. I was going to help her set aside the medicines she took...the vices that were killing her slowly. We were each other's safe harbor. Our lives were to be a grand adventure...and someone took that from us." Her eyes went from a whiskey-gold to a fiery amber as her features hardened behind her mask. "I am here to find out who it was."

"So am I," Mercy said with fierce determination, making another scan of the room, wondering if her killer was part of the revelry. "I wish Mathilde would have told me about you, Your Grace, it would be easier to believe your story. To be certain you had nothing to do with her death."

Felicity kicked her ankle.

"I understand," the Duchesse said around another melancholy sigh. "It is hard for us—*was* hard for us—as you might imagine. And because of where she came from...Mathilde did not trust easily."

"Of course it was difficult; people are not very understanding, are they?" Leaning over, Felicity placed her cobalt glove over that of the Duchesse. Sapphires over rubies. "I am sorry you lost your love."

Mercy allowed Felicity's endlessly romantic heart to soften her own toward the idea of the woman's innocence.

The Duchesse gave Felicity's fingers a grateful squeeze, then snatched her hand away. "Please do not be kind to me," she pled in a watery voice. "Not yet. I will have time to shatter into pieces of grief, but first she must be avenged."

Visibly grappling for her composure, Her Grace followed Mercy's gaze out toward the crowd. The revelers had taken on a fantastical quality, like a painted tableau or a moving picture. Vibrant, silken butterflies too frenetic to land.

Mercy put a thoughtful finger to the divot in her chin. "Do you wonder if your stepson has found out about the two of you and disapproved enough to be remonstrative?"

The Duchesse shook her head most violently. "Armand would never get his hands dirty, though he might have hired it done, a local ruffian, no doubt. I was trying to find out when..." She trailed off as something caught her attention.

It wasn't at all difficult to follow her gaze to exactly what had seized the Duchesse's notice.

Raphael Sauvageau demanded the consideration of any room he entered.

It was as if he claimed every plot of ground he trod upon, and dared someone to take it from him.

Mercy told herself that her heart only leapt because of the circumstance.

Not the man. Nor the sight of him in formal attire, his shoulders straight and jaw sharp.

Lucifer himself couldn't have been more devilishly handsome nor shrewd and savage than he, striding at the head of a handful of men who were nigh on nipping at his heels, as if his word, alone, held them on a short leash.

He approached a group of lads playing billiards. All of them, Mercy noted, were not fellows who easily wore white-tie finery, and yet each sported crimson carnations in their buttonholes.

"Do you know him?" Mercy asked the Duchesse.

"Who doesn't?" she replied ruefully. "I know he is playing a dangerous game tonight. That there are men here baying for his blood."

"What do you mean?" Mercy asked, unable to tear her eyes away from him.

The Duchesse shifted in her seat. "I overheard a conversation only moments ago between a man named Marco Villenueve and a Lord Longueville. Apparently, Mr. Sauvageau, he—how to say this?—he retracted a deal and blamed it on someone...a butcher?"

"The Butcher of High Street?" Felicity supplied with owl-wide eyes.

"Yes, yes, that's the one." The Duchesse nodded. "Everyone who stood around him looked as though they would have murdered him on the spot if they weren't in the public domain. He'd admitted to taking their money and sending it to Russia." She placed a hand at the base of her throat. "Russia, in this day and age? Madness."

Mercy suddenly understood what she was looking at. A tense conversation between the High Street Butchers—a particularly organized rival gang—and the King of the Fauves.

Her lover.

She tried superimposing the man who'd occupied her bed and body last night over the man who stood across the increasingly crowded billiards room.

He'd been rumpled and randy or, at times, tender and tentative. Touching her as if she were as delicate as one of the carnation petals he now plucked from the buttonhole of his enemy and crushed beneath his shoe.

What the devil was he thinking? That was tantamount to a public challenge to men like them, even *she* knew that.

Wars had been started over less insult.

"Lord Longueville is a dastardly man," Felicity offered, turning so she could covertly peek over her shoulder in the guise of a stretch. "I heard Father once called him a pustulant boil on the arse of the empire. He is said to have lost his fortune, and thereby became this Butcher of High Street. Why, I wonder, is Mr. Sauvageau challenging him?"

"It makes no sense. He's generally considered to be a suave and politic fellow..." The Duchesse trailed off again, her eyes narrowing on him. "I heard the men talking about moving against him the moment he leaves tonight. More will be outside the courtyard of his estate in wait for his Gabriel, who is a notorious recluse. I don't know him well, but I feel an odd sense of duty to warn him."

Felicity scrutinized the Duchesse. "Why would you feel a duty to—"

"I'll do it." Mercy stood so quickly, she became a bit lightheaded, whether from the heat of the crowded manse or the sudden pounding of her heart, she couldn't be sure.

She blinked away the sensation before all but yanking Felicity out of her seat.

"You and the Duchesse should go for the authorities without alerting anyone. I think there will be violence here tonight."

"Erm..." Felicity gulped and looked at the floor, her face flushing behind her mask.

"What is it?"

"Don't be angry."

A pang of anxiety thrummed deep in her stomach. *"Felicity."*

"I engaged an errand boy before we left, and sent a note to Morley the moment we arrived."

"What?" She forced the word out through clenched teeth.

Felicity put her hands up as if to ward off a blow. Or a gunshot. "I know you didn't want that, but, Mercy, it was foolhardy for us to walk into such a situation without anyone knowing where we are. The moment we arrived I sensed danger, and who better to turn to than our reasonable and protective brother-in-law?"

"Felicity, you have no idea what you've done." Mercy threw her hands in the air. "Morley is still obligated to take Raphael into custody."

"Raphael? Why would you be worried about..." Felicity cocked her head in a very sparrow-like gesture.

"You say his name as if you're acquainted. Mercy, are the two of you...involved?"

Oh Lord. She was entirely unprepared to answer a question of that scope. "No! Well... Yes. That is —I—we—"

"Mon Dieu." The Duchesse covered her mouth. "You're in love with him."

"I never!" The protest rang false, even to her own ears.

She felt rather than saw the Duchesse lift a dubious eyebrow from behind her mask. "Lovers, then?"

Mercy's lips slammed together. She couldn't bring herself to deny it. To lie. And yet, how could she explain? If he was involved with Mathilde, then would the poor grieving Duchesse have her heart broken all over again to hear of it?

"You *made love* to the man arrested for Mathilde's murder?" It was Felicity's eyes that carried the gravest of wounds. "And worse, you didn't tell me?"

It was the first secret ever kept between them.

Mercy took her twin's hand. "I met him in front of the wolf exhibit yesterday and he asked if he could come to me... I—I couldn't resist him. And also, I couldn't bring myself to talk about it. Not when things are so complicated. But I promise you I'm not being sentimental when I tell you that I know he's innocent of this crime. I have evidence."

Felicity pulled her hand away. "But he's guilty of a thousand other crimes! Or don't you remember the night he might have *killed* us for the gold Nora's late husband stole from him?"

"He gave that to Titus and Nora's hospital," Mercy pointed out.

"It was no gift. He said he'd collect on the balance, remember? I think of that every day. What sort of debt Honoria and Titus might find themselves beholden to?

When will he come for our sister?"

"He won't." Mercy's defense of him sounded pallid and desperate, even to her own ears. "He wants out of the Fauves. The gang was his father's, and he was born to this life, but his plan is to leave it all behind."

To leave her behind.

She turned to the Duchesse. "I suspect that has something to do with his reckless behavior tonight. I think...I think he might be trying to destroy what his father built."

"Mercy, you're speaking madness!" Felicity shook her a little.

"No...she's not," the Duchesse shocked them both into silence with her words. "Gabriel and Raphael Sauvageau's father was known as *le Bourreau*. The executioner. He was said to have been an Englishman of some renown, though no one knew his identity. He was infamous in Monaco and France, indeed, all over the Mediterranean. I know that he used his family awfully, and broke his eldest son in the fighting pits."

Felicity wrapped her arms around her middle, shaking her head in disbelief. "How do you know all this?"

Mercy wondered that as well.

The Duchesse's chin gave a tremulous wobble. "Because *le Bourreau* hurt Mathilde. Showed her...unnatural affections when she was just a girl, even though she was the daughter of his wife's sister, Patrice."

Mercy gasped in horror for poor Mathilde. "You mean..."

"Yes, Mathilde and Raphael are—*were* cousins. This is why I feel some duty toward him. He is a ruthless man, to be sure, but he was kind to her. Even when kindness was never a part of that awful dynasty."

Cousins.

Not lovers.

That was why Raphael had come to see Mathilde on the day she died. Why he was so fond of her without professing any romantic relationships.

It was why he was so intent upon finding her killer.

Because they were family.

She turned back to the billiards table to find that he'd disappeared, though their men were still at each other's throats.

Damn but that was an irritating skill of his. Slithering away just when she needed to talk to him.

"I have to find him. To warn him. Whatever he has planned tonight, he has to stop it."

Felicity grabbed for her as she fled away, but missed. "Mercy, no!"

"You were right, Felicity, to send for Morley. You must go find him now. Must tell him there is a war brewing in this very house that might spill onto the streets of London, and then go home where it's safe."

With that, Mercy turned and plunged through a crowd of drunken crowing lads, intent upon searching every room in the house until he turned up.

Oh, when she caught up with him, he'd have more than a few things to answer for. Just how did he plan on finding Mathilde's killer when he was busy stirring discontent between dangerous people?

Didn't he understand he was putting himself in undue danger?

Just as she was elbowing through the crowd at the doorway to the ballroom, a strong hand seized said elbow and yanked her toward the dance floor.

One minute she was walking. The next she was waltzing, and the transition had been so seamlessly elegant and effortless, it could only have been perpetrated by one arrogant rake.

"What the everlasting *fuck* are you doing here?" Raphael snarled against her ear, even as he encircled her in an embrace that could only be considered protective.

Mercy hated that dancing in his arms was about as exhilarating as flying. That she thrilled at every press of his thigh against hers and every subtle flex of his arm or his shoulder as he led her through the steps to the dizzying waltz.

She tried not to notice that his nostrils flared when he was angry, and beneath a mask that seemed to be made of dark serpentine scales, each furious breath was rather endearing.

"What do you think?" She tossed her head with brash irreverence, daring him to dress her down. "I'm looking for Mathilde's murderer! Which is what you should be doing instead of—"

"I thought we agreed you'd leave that to me." His fingers almost bit into her back as he pulled her indecently close to avoid being clobbered by a drunken couple.

"You *assumed* I'd leave it to you," she bit back, finding herself reluctant to regain a proper distance, regardless of her ire. "*I agreed* to take my further findings to the police, which I will now that I have further findings. I didn't before, and so no agreement between us was breached."

He opened his mouth to reply, and she beat him to it, cutting off any incoming homilies.

"Listen to this." She squeezed the mound of his coiled bicep in her excitement. "I spoke to the Duchesse de la Cour, who claims she wasn't after Mathilde but about to run away with her. They were lovers, if you'll believe it."

He didn't miss a step, but remained silent for an entire refrain of music, as if he didn't know which part of their conversation to address first.

"Mathilde...with a woman? I always thought it was

Marco..." he muttered.

"Who?"

"My second in command who was placed by my father before his death. He's the one most likely to turn on me when—" He paused. "It doesn't matter. I do know that Mathilde procured most of her vice from Marco. Often those arrangements are...physical. I know she'd angered him lately, and I intended to wrest a confession from him tonight."

She glowered up at his impossibly handsome, aggravating face. "And you kept that tidbit of information from me? How dare you!"

The look he sent back to her threatened to immolate her on the spot.

Not because it was angry.

Quite the opposite. It was possibly the most tender, honest gaze she'd ever received in her lifetime. "I would die before I put you in the path of a man like Marco Villenueve... The Good Book says never to cast your pearls before swine."

"Yes, well, it also says never to eat shellfish, and I had a cracking huge lobster last night."

He barked out a harsh, caustic laugh that did nothing to soften the pinched lines of worry casting his features into stark and savage relief. "I don't know whether to be delighted or infuriated with you."

"While you make up your mind, hear this," she plunged ahead. "The Duchesse thinks possibly a member of her ducal family might have hired an assassin once they found out about their plans to leave together. So, you see, you can't start a gang war right now because we're so close to finding your cousin's killer, Raphael." She paused for a moment to glare up at him. "By the by, don't for *one minute* think you've gotten away with implying that you two were—"

She made a plaintive squeak as he spun her off the

floor with such force, they stumbled toward a hall beneath the grand stairs, parting the crowd, unconcerned with another drunken couple stumbling around.

"Where are we going?" she huffed, trying to dig her heels in as he dragged her toward a simple, unadorned entry that branched from the main room.

"I'm getting you out of here safely...so I can throttle you in peace," he said from between teeth that his coiled jaw wouldn't allow to separate. "Goddammit, Mercy, you have no idea what you've done."

CHAPTER 14

*M*ercy wriggled, jerked, and flopped about, but was unable to break Raphael's relentless grip as he tirelessly dragged her up a dark set of spiraling stairs and into a deserted passageway. "How dare you manhandle me, you ignominious arse!"

"I've been called worse," he muttered as he pinned her to his side with one arm, to test several door handles. Finding one unlocked, he shoved her inside and followed in, slamming the door shut.

"Oh, no you don't! I am not about to be tossed into some—" Just where were they?

Mercy paused to look around their dim surroundings, noting the two small, bare, if neatly made beds, open trunks, and matching spare-looking wardrobes. Unused maids' chambers, it seemed. Which would explain why the entire part of the house was abandoned, overcome as the staff would be during such an affair as this. They'd be below stairs where the kitchens were located, along with the male servants' quarters.

Raphael slid the lock on the door and blocked it with all six feet of hard, infuriated male.

The only light filtered in through the thin windows above the beds, provided by several lanterns in the garden. It slanted over him at just such an angle, casting half his features in light and the other half in shadow.

As if the two battled over him.

Mercy stood fast, planting her feet shoulder-width apart so as not to advertise how the very sight of him made her weak in the knees. "I don't know what you think you're doing but I demand—"

"I'm saving you from your own recklessness!"

Mercy was certain the look in his eyes might have caused any number of men to tremble, to surrender. But she would not be cowed.

And God help her, she refused to surrender.

Not again.

"Don't be absurd," she scoffed. "If anything, *I'm* saving *you*. I can't believe you told Lord Longueville, one of the worst men alive, that you took his money. Do you know his enemies disappear in the night? He's in league with the High Street Butchers! Not only will he be after you, but so will that rather dodgy fellow— Marco was it—that works for you. The Duchesse said they were baying for your blood. Not to mention the police are—"

He lunged forward, as if to seize her, but at the last moment, he snatched his arms back, his fists clenched so tightly the creases turned white. "I wasn't supposed to be saved tonight, you *magnificent* fool."

"What?"

She'd seen those stark, savage hazel eyes turn every possible color depending on the light. His emotion. His intention.

But never like this. Flashing with twin lightning bolts in the half dark. Then gathering with thunderous grey clouds.

A storm approached, and it was about to break over them both.

"You think I didn't know *exactly* what I was doing?"

He sliced the air between them with the flat of his hand. "I know that the Butchers and Lord Longueville are working together. I know they approached Marco, and that Marco failed to tell me, which means he's already mounted a mutiny of the Fauves against me. The Fauves would have dumped my body at the bloody door of Buckingham Palace and Longueville and his Butchers would have strung me from Hangman's Dock. Either way these streets were to be my grave tonight."

"Wait..." Everything inside her went unnaturally still. She stood in the eye of the storm, searching him for the truth. "You're *serious*," she realized with a jolt. "You were intending to perish tonight? To actually die? As in...not exist any longer?"

She waited for him to deny it. Which he would, certainly. Any moment now.

The expression on his face stole her hope before he even formulated a reply.

"My plan calls for a martyr," he explained in a tone devoid of emotion. "The Fauves still loyal to me will seek vengeance against Marco and his traitors. The Butchers will, no doubt, take advantage of the chaos and rise up to swallow the battling factions whole. The Blackheart of Ben More and Morley won't allow for such pandemonium, and I've anonymously provided enough evidence to search Longueville's estate, where they'll find what they need to stretch his neck. And I'll be goddamned if you're here to be any part of it. There *is* a war coming, Mercy, and you need to get out before it starts."

She scowled at him. "You're mad!"

Threading fingers through his hair, he snarled, "What I am, is desperate."

"I meant you're insane if you think I'm leaving you now. Someone has to keep you from killing yourself, you bleeding idiot."

He seemed to search the night for something, any-thing, to convince her. "What about the Duchesse and Mathilde? Who will crack the case after I am gone?"

Crossing her arms, she raked him with her most imperious glare. "You're going nowhere, Raphael Sauvageau, I'll not allow it."

"You can't stop me, Mercy. It's already done," he insisted.

"That doesn't mean it can't be undone!"

Seizing her, he bent so their eyes were close, his boring the reflection of the moon into her very soul with palpable agony. "You think I want this? It's the only way out. The only way *Gabriel lives*. When my corpse is found, so too will be Gabriel's mask. Dr. Con-leith is hard at work this very evening, sorting out his injured face. The Fauves will assume we are both gone, and my brother can finally live with his new identity."

Titus was in on this? Did Nora know?

"No." She wrenched away, whirling so she didn't have to face him. "I don't accept this."

"Wouldn't you give your life for your sister?"

His question landed like a dagger in her back.

"Of course, I would! But there has to be some other way. Can you not have a new identity as well?"

"I'm too well known. I've too much money, infamy, and the men beneath me happen to be wealthy enough to search for ages, because as much as I've hated it, I'm damn good at what I do."

She could feel him getting closer, and wished her knees didn't go weak at his proximity.

"The world is only getting smaller, Mercy, and I would be found eventually. I have contacts in every port. I've either swindled or smuggled for half the known world, and to truly go into hiding, we'd have to find some place off a map, where the only thing to do is make our own swill and buggar local livestock. I'm not going to live like that. And I don't want that for my brother. He's already suffered enough. And..."

He broke off and they were both silent as footsteps plodded by. Someone opened a door to the next room and rustled around in it before heading back the other way, muttering about apron straps and extra mending.

"*And what?*" Mercy demanded when they were again safely alone.

"I've lived enough for two lifetimes."

"No, you haven't. No!" She shoved at him. "I'll not allow it, you selfish bastard."

"Calm down, someone will hear you." He gently encircled her shoulders with soothing fingers, but she jerked away.

"I will not calm down!" She paced a few feet toward the bare walls and then spun back to him "Why did you kiss me then, if you were just going to do this? Why make love to me? Why the devil would you make me...make me care for you?"

His features collapsed then. Broke open like a shattered glass. "I kissed you, Mercy, because I knew your taste would be better than any last meal I could devise. I made love to you because I *am* a selfish bastard, and I wanted a glimpse of what heaven would be like before I join the ranks of the damned. I thought you knew better than to care. That you understood I don't deserve it."

Mercy didn't realize what was welling inside of her until her hand flung out and struck him on the cheek.

God, that was satisfying.

The pain.

The blank look of shock on the beautiful bastard's face.

Heat swirled inside her. A conflagration of rage fed by helplessness and...and something else. Something so

169

profound and breathtaking it threatened to turn her to ash.

She wanted to scream at the idea of his loss. His death. This vital, tender, brilliant villain. This man who would dismantle his father's tainted legacy for the love of his brother.

Who would give his life.

She slapped him again. Harder this time. Apparently unable to control herself at the tragic thought of his demise.

His head flinched ever so slightly to the side, but he said nothing. Did nothing. Took her fury on the chin while those bleak, abysmal, exquisite eyes threatened to destroy her with the agony she read in their depths.

She pulled her hand back once more, the sting from her previous strike having yet to fade. Words tumbled into her throat, but she couldn't seem to speak them. Not to the face of the man who was the specter of every wicked dream she'd dared to remember.

The answer to every question she'd not known to ask.

The only reason she'd consider abandoning her vow to remain alone.

That thought stole her breath as she stared at him in mute wonder.

He'd the body of a man, and the soul of a beast. An animal's primitive instinct. And it summoned something so ancient and powerful from the deepest parts of her. Something needful and violent, carnal and famished. He teased and tantalized her. Amused and antagonized her.

And the entire time he was planning his own death.

She had meant to slap him again, she really had. To strike the very idea out of his head.

It was impossible to discern who lunged first.

His muscles twitched, hers responded, or the other way around, it wasn't relevant in the end.

When their bodies crashed together like waves finding their own shore, all that mattered was that their lips finally met. Savored. Punished. Pleaded.

Devoured. Consumed.

Her fingers bracketed the rough skin of his jaw, a lovely tactile dichotomy to the smoothness of his lips.

Like silk and sand.

The kiss did not douse the flames of fury within her, merely fed them, fanned them, sent the heat licking its way over her flesh until it landed deep inside her womb.

Her snarl of demand somehow escaped as a whimper of need.

She was dimly aware of a sense of weightlessness and a rush of air before she found herself pinned on her back to a mattress.

Above her, Raphael's teeth bared and his eyes glinted with a dangerous hunger. He caught her wrists and effortlessly held them in one large hand, securing them above her head.

He descended on her then, a low growl erupting from him as he dragged his mouth everywhere. Her jaw, her neck, the angle of her clavicle before returning to her lips to start a different trail.

Vibrations of heat and hunger shook her to her very bones as a terrific heaviness gathered in her loins. She found herself astonished that a kiss might convey more than words. She felt the unrequited need, the loveless lifetime of desolation.

He was not gentle as he'd been the night before. The tender, skillful lover had been replaced by this savage, cruel beast. He used his teeth, nipping at tender skin and then smoothing it over with the hot velvet of his tongue.

Even though he was heavy enough to crush her, some fervency rose within her, telling her she'd never get close enough. Not matter how deep he went.

She opened her legs, intent upon locking her ankles around his back, clinging to him like the pathetic barnacle he'd made of her. She pressed up against him, grinding at the turgid barrel of his erection through the damnable barrier of their clothing.

His brutal sound was her only warning before she found herself shoved face down on the mattress. Rough hands pulled her hips up and back, and the whisper of fabric foreshadowed the crisp air hitting the warm skin of her upper thighs as he shoved her skirts above her back.

Her drawers gave nothing but a sigh of protest as he ripped them, and the raw sound he made as his fingers found the backs of her garters released a flood of desire from the very core of her.

He split her with his finger, testing the flesh already slick and eager.

Willing.

Her fingers twisted in the rough wool blanket beneath her, she arched her back toward a sudden, intense onslaught of need.

His hand gripped her bare hip and after a few jerking motions, he was there. The blunt head of his cock kissing the folds guarding her sex.

He stilled then, his grip on the flesh of her hip bruising as the only sound in the night was the rasp of his panting breaths.

"Damn you," he finally snarled. "Damn you for..."

For what?

She never had the chance to ask.

He drove inside her with one searing, merciless thrust. Penetrating not just her body, but searing her very soul.

There was a momentary sharp pain as flesh still tender from the previous night struggled to contain him once again.

Biting her lip, Mercy forced herself not to gasp, because she wanted this. Needed it. Craved the violence of this storm between them. She threw her head back and pressed her body toward him. Taking him impossibly deeper. Until the bones of his hips met the soft flesh of her ass.

With a low, appreciative sound, he set a rhythm as relentless as he was. His cock parting her, filling her, injecting her with currents of lightning-quick pleasure as he drove so deep, she thought at times he caressed her womb.

She could feel his heartbeat inside of her as her intimate muscles gripped and goaded him with lugubrious tension, unwilling to release him each time he withdrew.

He gripped her dress, holding it like the reins of a horse as he drove deep and hard, bucking her forward with the force of his thrusts. He held her captive as he undid her completely.

Mercy said his name. Then she screamed it.

Bending over her, his hand reached around and covered her mouth.

She could taste her own slick desire on his skin, and she bit into the rough pads of his fingers as he crippled her with release. Relentless spasms uncoiled within her, thundering through her veins with such astounding force she couldn't help but bear down against the overwhelming bliss.

An inhuman sound tore from him, then another, as his impressive muscles locked into a jerking tempo.

His cock swelled impossibly larger inside of her the moment before a rushing jet of warmth bathed her womb, heightening her own climax until stars danced in her periphery, threatening to steal her consciousness.

And why not? He was a consummate thief, after all.

She'd never offered him her heart.

But he'd taken it all the same.

CHAPTER 15

*D*amn her.

Damn her for making him feel more alive than he ever had, on the night he was supposed to die. For teaching him what hope felt like. For making him wonder what a future might be.

Damn her for changing everything. His plans. His mind.

His heart.

What was happening? He'd been a man of absolute resolve and relentless, one-minded orientation until *this* whirlwind of a woman touched down in his life.

She challenged everything he'd known to be true.

It was more impossible between them now than it had ever been. His machinations were a runaway train charging down a steep mountain.

Chased by an avalanche.

There was no stopping it.

Time was of the essence, and yet he couldn't bring himself to bloody withdraw from the velvet warmth of her body, even long after the earth-shattering climax had passed.

How could he leave the world she inhabited? It'd somehow become impossible. Unthinkable.

Because she cared. She'd admitted it with those lustrous blue eyes gone dark with anger tempered only by desire. Anger precipitated by the pain of his loss.

Other than his brother, he couldn't think of another person alive that would mourn him.

Until Mercy.

She was the one to pull away and detach, bringing him plummeting back to reality with a jarring crash.

She rolled to her back and he turned away, righting himself as he allowed her the privacy to do the same.

"Well, I hope that settles things," she said after a moment of rustling fabric, her crisp tone rasping over the afterglow of satisfied lust.

He wished he felt the same.

Things were more unsettled than ever.

And his need for her would never be satisfied. Not if he lived another hundred years.

Gathering his fortitude, he turned back to her in time to see that she'd tidied herself with her ruined undergarments and stood, balling them up in her grasp.

"These are for the rubbish." She set about looking for a bin. Finding one, she dropped them inside before catching her reflection in the mirror and smoothing her hair back into place.

Was there ever a woman more precious? This force of nature in a petite, golden package. His fierce vixen. Not merely gorgeous but adventurous. Stimulating. Magnificent.

He was used to making a stir wherever he went, but if she were ever to throw off the mantle of civility thrust upon her by her family, by society, her rank...

She'd eclipse him with a brilliance to shame the sun.

He'd never wanted anything more than to witness such a thing.

Sweet Christ, they'd never even taken off their masks.

And now she'd be moving around the earth with those flimsy garters holding up her sheer stockings and no drawers.

The very idea was enough to make him ready to have her again.

Mayhem erupted beneath them. Cries and whistles screeched over the sounds of doors splintering open and the clatter of wagons thundering up the drive.

"What the bloody devil?" He raced to the door and opened it, glancing down the hall to see if the ruckus had reached their deserted corner of the manse.

A few footsteps thundered down the narrow stairs, but only the skirts of frightened maids appeared before they dashed by.

"Oh, dear."

Closing the door, he turned to the woman who'd uttered the words, with slow, deliberate movements.

She offered him a smile of chagrin. "That...sounds like Morley and his men."

Raphael hurled a few choice French curses into the night, and she held her hands up as if to block them from landing on her.

"Before you get angry with me, I wasn't the one who summoned the police. That was Felicity. She did it without my consent and, believe you me, no one was more cross about that than I. But in the end, it's a good thing because—"

"Felicity?" He advanced toward her, his heart thundering in his ears. "Tell me she's not downstairs in *that*."

Mercy shook her head. "As soon as we realized what you were about—and how many dangerous men were here—I sent her to meet Morley. He'd surely have made certain she was safe."

"Good." He seized her, planted a quick, hard kiss to her bruised lips. "I'll clear you a path to him, but you must stay here."

"And *you* must be joking." She wrenched away from him and strode toward the door. "I'm not hiding up here when the Duchesse is caught up in the bedlam."

He caught her elbow. "Any number of those men are not above taking hostages to escape the police. There are innocent people threaded throughout a labyrinth of warring factions. And, as you said, most of them are out for my blood. How am I supposed to concentrate on the task at hand if you're in danger?"

"I'm not harmless, I'll have you know." Her jaw thrust forward as she reached into her sleeve and produced an impressive-looking knife. "Do you really think I'd trust a suicidal gangster to set things to right? Not bloody likely, I'll take my chances down there, thank you."

"But—"

She gave her golden curls a saucy toss. "No one knows of our...connection. So if someone comes for your throat, I'll simply step aside and let them have at you, and it'd be what you deserve."

As she flounced away, one knee-weakening truth became unerringly obvious.

He was in trouble.

No.

He...was in love.

To him, the emotion hadn't been definable. He'd never truly stopped to ponder it. Just accepted that he felt something like it for his brother. Had done so once for his mother.

Not that his emotions for Mercy were anything filial. Indeed, he hated to admit they might be stronger even in so short a time.

He'd known he'd loved Gabriel because his brother meant more than himself. Because he'd die for him. Kill for him. His loyalty was absolute and unquestioned.

But for Mercy?

He'd burn the entire world to the ground if she asked him. He'd accomplish any Herculean task. Sail to the ends of the world to fetch a trinket she liked.

He not only loved her enough to stay if it were possible.

He loved her enough to let her go if it meant keeping her safe.

The realization galvanized him forward as she wrenched the door open and plunged into the hall.

He hovered behind her like the very wrath of God, brandishing his own sharp dagger as they spiraled back down the stairs. Raphael searched for another way out, but the only entrance and exit to this specific tower dumped them right toward the main hall of the keep.

Damn these old fortresses.

He lunged around her as they struggled through the short corridor toward the great hall, gathering her free hand in his. "You'll stay glued to me, Mercy, or so help me God!"

To his surprise and utter relief, she nodded in compliance.

Keeping her latched between him and the wall, Raphael shoved past bodies who'd begun to flee down whichever hall they could find, not knowing they raced toward a dead end.

An acrid smell itched at his nose, smoke and something bitter.

He snatched a panicked footman clean off his feet. "What's going on out there?" he demanded.

"Madness!" The gawky lad's voice squeaked with the fear of a man barely out of his teenage years. "Someone spied the Bobbies and before we knew it, a tussle broke out right on the ballroom floor. Men at each other's throats. Never seen anything like it. Someone tossed over an oil lamp and now the drapes in the gaming den have caught. Best we run, man."

Cursing, Raphael released him and shouldered his way to the end of the hall.

He took a quick toll of the anarchy when they broke onto the landing that wrapped around the great room's second story, at eye level with the ostentatious chandelier.

Morley's men spilled into the courtyard like blue-coated rats. Some doing their best to contain the tide of panicked partygoers, funneling them out to safety.

Others brandished an asp to meet the blows of gangster cudgels.

Longueville was nowhere to be found, and without him and Raphael to maintain the temperature on the simmering tension between the Fauves and the Butchers, it had boiled over into this potentially lethal catastrophe.

It wasn't supposed to have happened this way. Only the leaders and their closest comrades were to meet here and witness his challenge.

Then they'd gather their men to come after him in the night.

That was how things were done in their world. They were no street-rat ruffians, their wars were waged in the dark so there were no witnesses.

Away from the public and the police.

But Longueville had blatantly brought an army to a masquerade, willing to crush revelers if necessary.

The rules of engagement had been thoroughly breached.

Two staircases led down to the ballroom floor, one on the east wall and the other on the west.

Raphael and Mercy weaved through abandoned card games and a fortune teller's upended table toward the west staircase as a fight began to spill up the east side toward the second floor.

"The Duchesse was in the billiard's room when last I

saw her!" Mercy called over the din. "There!" She pointed to a large solarium now crammed with people trying to escape the smoke beginning to seep up through the three open archways.

Raphael nodded, his eyes lasering everything else away but a bold figure who'd led the police charge into the courtyard. He already had two Butchers in irons and was dragging them roughly toward a police cart very much like the one in which Raphael had first kissed Mercy.

Chief Inspector Morley.

He'd get Mercy to him before returning for the Duchesse.

Her safety was paramount to anything else.

Cursing every fucking god in existence, Raphael tucked Mercy deeper against his side, readied his weapon, and waded into the fray. He was careful to keep his dagger away from drunken, panicked courtesans, artists, and actresses as they shoved and fled.

Keeping to the outskirts, he hoped to avoid the increasing intensity of the violence in the great room. Once on the main floor, he had no qualms about using his elbows, fists, or his blade to quell any who came close. Who thought to claim bragging rights by landing a blow against Raphael Sauvageau.

He had one eye on the brawl and the other on the exit that remained infuriatingly distant, when he felt Mercy lunge behind them.

Raphael whirled just in time to see her blade embedded in the chest of one of his own men, who'd apparently thought to attack from behind.

They thought to stab him in the back. Thinking, no doubt, that he wouldn't see it coming, this coup against the rules of conflict.

Because he'd taught them the code and abided by it.

But Marco...he didn't have a code. He would conduct his villainy out in the open, if only to amass the notoriety the Sauvageau brothers had taken a lifetime to procure.

Raphael would see him in hell, but first...

Gaining ground, he stopped an attacker with a swift elbow to the throat. He threw his dagger at another man who had a running start. It embedded in his eye, dropping him instantly.

Now Raphael was weaponless, but it didn't matter, he only had five paces to the door and sharp fucking knuckles.

Anyone in his way had a death wish. The peal of a woman's scream rose above the din, the desperation in the sound seeming to slow time itself.

"Felicity! She didn't leave in time!"

Raphael had to employ both hands to stop Mercy from lunging through the brawl toward the far staircase.

Where Marco Villeneuve fought against the crowd of tussling men, his arm around the waist of a struggling, petite woman Mercy's exact likeness in feature and formal gown.

Felicity's mask had been torn away and her hair ruined by the cruel hand threaded through it, using the pain of his grasp to subdue her.

Tears streamed down cheeks frozen in a heart-wrenching mask of panic that Raphael could never even imagine painted on Mercy's resolute features.

"We have to get to her!" Mercy cried, her own expression more temper than terror.

Felicity spotted them across the crowd, and the sight seemed to inject her with courage. As close as they were to the fire, Felicity's struggles produced violent coughs that interrupted her sobs. However, she landed a lucky blow with her elbow into Marco's sharp jaw.

Stunned, Marco released her.

Only to spin her around and deliver a merciless blow with the back of his hand.

Felicity dropped beneath the fray, disappearing from view.

An inhuman roar brought Raphael's notice to the top of the stairs.

What he saw slackened his limbs with shock.

Mercy chose that moment to lunge so frantically toward her sister, and he almost lost his grip. "Let me go!" she screamed. "I will murder that man!"

"You won't have to," he said, strengthening his grip on her, pointing to the top of the stairs.

Gabriel was unmistakable, even in a lupine mask Raphael had never seen before. He charged down the stairs toward Marco. What men were not tossed over the banister became little better than smears on the wall.

To Marco's credit, he stood against the oncoming juggernaut, pulling a knife from his belt.

A shot from the direction of the door brought time to an absolute standstill. Everyone screamed and the collective crowd ducked, subsequently checking themselves for wounds.

"Are you struck?" Raphael grasped Mercy, gripped with horror. "Dammit, are you all right?"

"I'm unharmed," she said, her voice shaking and small.

Raphael checked the entry for the shooter but could identify none.

When he looked back toward the stairs to find that Gabriel had disappeared in the thickening smoke, he felt as though the bullet had found his own chest.

Marco was reaching down to collect Felicity, who'd yet to recover from his blow.

Raphael wheezed out his brother's name just in time

to watch him rise from behind the banister like the very specter of the black-swathed reaper.

Gabriel and Marco both lashed out at the same time, one with his blade, the other with nothing more than a scarred fist the size of a sledgehammer.

Gabriel's punch connected with an audibly satisfying crunch of bone, though Marco's knife barely missed the eye he'd aimed it for.

By the time the traitorous Spaniard finished rolling arse-over-end to land in a twisted heap, Gabriel had stooped to retrieve Felicity from where she'd been draped unconscious on the stairs.

Raphael's eyes burned, his throat closed over with emotion.

Not with relief.

With horror.

Horror that echoed in the gasps and exclamations of the congregation before leaping out of Gabriel's way as he carried the young Baron's daughter like a bolt of cobalt cloth.

Marco's knife had missed his brother's flesh, but it'd cut his mask away.

Exposing his face to everyone.

Gabriel kept his chin held high, relentlessly marched forward, using his monstrous appearance to part the sea of people still ebbing toward the door.

Raphael surged forward, shoving through the crowd, knowing he'd get Mercy to safety.

Trusting his brother to save Felicity.

He could see through the doors ahead that Morley had tossed his prisoners into the police wagon. Just in time to catch a sobbing woman with a bloodied nose as she collapsed.

Raphael had half-expected the Chief Inspector to have fired the shot, as he was a famous marksman, but there was no way he could have done it.

He was simply too far away.

Just as they were about to break free of the castle's threshold, a figure lunged from around the corner and kicked out at Mercy's legs.

She gave a sharp cry of pain, and went sprawling onto her hands and knees.

Striking like a venomous cobra, Raphael had the man's throat in a vice grip before anyone could react. "You'll die for that," he vowed, reaching down with his other hand to lift Mercy off the ground.

"So says the dead man walking." Even over the deafening chaos, the unmistakable click of a pistol washed Raphael's veins in ice.

"Think you can knock me down and get away with it?" sneered former Detective Inspector Martin Trout, his face still a tapestry of purple and yellow healing bruises. "Unhand me, or I pull the trigger."

Raphael's hands ached for the feel of Trout's thin bones breaking beneath them. He would pick his teeth with this man. Would make him choke to death on his own genitals for daring to touch her.

Something inside ignited, engulfing those pushing for escape in a billow of smoke.

The crowd rushed the door with renewed vigor. Bodies flowed around them as if they were stones in a rushing river, heavy enough to not be swept up in the current, but in danger of being swallowed by it.

If Raphael moved, Mercy might be trampled.

She gasped his name and tugged at his sleeve, having yet to regain her feet. The pain she valiantly tried to hide from her voice lanced through his chest. "Raphael, his boots!"

Raphael looked down to see the barrel of the gun aimed not as his middle, but Mercy's head. And below even that.

Were Brogan boots with an uncommonly tall heel.

Like one a detective of dubious height might buy to enhance his stature.

The soles of which had left muddy footprints beneath Mathilde Archambeau's window when he crept in to murder her.

"It was you!" Mercy snarled, a fierce woman even on her knees. "You cretinous pig."

Raphael released the man's neck with the greatest reluctance, knowing a fear he'd never imagined possible at the sight of a pistol about to kiss the temple of his woman.

"Just a hired gun, so to speak," Trout corrected, oozing with antipathy and malevolence. "Spoiled French aristocrats pay better than the English government to punish their scandalous stepmothers. Better, even, than the High Street Butchers."

"If you shoot now, you'll be found out." Raphael nodded in Morley's direction. "You can't murder the Chief Inspector's sister-in-law when he's right across the courtyard."

Trout grinned. "This is all laid at your feet, and people see what we tell them to see, which is the King of the Fauves killing a Baron's daughter and me wrestling the gun from you to put you down. I'll emerge from the fire a bloody hero. Your fucking brother-in-law will likely pin the medal on my jacket himself." His finger caressed the trigger. "I thought that woman on the stairs was you," he spat. "Don't worry, I won't miss a second time."

CHAPTER 16

From Mercy's perspective, Raphael moved with such incredible speed, the rest of the world slowed in comparison.

One moment she was staring down the barrel of the instrument of her death.

And the next, he'd seized the pistol by said barrel, wrenched it toward his own middle, and twisted it out of Trout's hands before another shot could be fired.

He didn't shoot the man, as she thought a generally unscrupulous gangster such as he might do.

Rather—with his demonic features made even more so by his mask—the violence he perpetrated on Trout with the butt of the pistol no doubt left the man wishing for death.

If he didn't succumb to it.

She wasn't sure a man could survive such a savage beating.

She wasn't sure she cared.

A crimson mask blocked her view just as she was coming to liken the odious detective's face to the ground meat inside sausage casings.

"Are you hurt?" The Duchesse pulled at her elbow, lifting her to her feet.

Mercy stared at her dumbly. Was she hurt? The opposite, it seemed. She felt no pain whatsoever. She couldn't feel her fingers or her lips. Perhaps she gestured in the negative, but she couldn't tell.

"That man was hired by Armand to kill Mathilde," Mercy said in a rather matter-of-fact way.

The woman's kind eyes hardened. "That is exactly Armand's way. He often turns to the corrupt officials to do his bidding." She ripped off her mask, whirled, and spat on him, stepping on his neck with the sharp heel of her bejeweled boot.

"You break her neck, I break yours."

And she did.

Dimly, Mercy was aware of Raphael's strong arms sweeping her away, of following a burgundy gown back into a burning building.

"Felicity!" She dug in her heels, searching the increasingly smoke-clogged room for her sister.

In all the chaos, she hadn't witnessed her sister's escape, and considering who was carrying Felicity, it wasn't likely she'd have missed it. He was head and shoulders taller than most men.

"Many of us took pleasure barges and gondolas to get here," the Duchesse said over her shoulder. "I directed your sister and Gabriel to the tunnel beneath the keep that will take us to the canal where my boat is waiting."

That roused Mercy from her stupor better than anything else she could imagine might do. *Felicity.* Her guileless sister was a stranger to violence. So sweet-natured and timid was she, no one ever even entertained the notion of striking her.

They hurried by torchlight through the thousand-year-old tunnel toward the sound of water lapping at the stone docks. Voices ahead of them advertised that others had come this way in search of their boats, and what that meant for her sister, Mercy couldn't imagine.

A strange birdlike whistle from the dark caused Raphael to tense and freeze beside her.

Veering to the left, Raphael went toward an alcove that branched off the main causeway; Mercy and the Duchesse followed quickly on his heels.

They found Gabriel sitting with his back against the stones, hood pulled low over his face, those startling, abysmal shadows swallowing the horror of his features from view.

Cradled in his massive arms, Felicity looked like a child rather than a woman of twenty.

His fingers hovered over the place above her cheekbone where a raw mark formed.

Pale lashes cast shadows over her cheeks, and Mercy made a raw sound of relief to see them tremble.

She rushed to her sister, sinking down next to the giant of a man to take her cold, limp hand. "Felicity, can you hear me?"

"She woke." The graveled voice came from the void behind the hood. "She opened her eyes, said your name, and...and looked at me..."

A bleak note underscored his words with abject desolation.

"She faints when she's..." Mercy cut off, realizing the man had spoken in perfect English.

"When she's terrified," he finished.

Raphael had mentioned before that Gabriel did not speak English. No doubt, it was a truth they hid from the world.

"I don't have her smelling salts." She tapped Felicity on the uninjured cheek. "Darling, can you come around? Do you hear me?"

"Some cold water from the canal, maybe?" the Duchesse suggested, tearing the hem of her dress. "I'll soak this and put it against her neck, that might do the trick."

A resourceful woman, the Duchesse.

Raphael loomed over them, both a comforting presence and a frightening specter of wrath splattered by the blood of his enemy.

He glared daggers down at his brother. "Why are you not being carved into by Dr. Conleith right now?"

The face in the shadow of the hood didn't lift, but shifted away from her, answering in French. "Because, *mon frere*, I went to the surgeon's table thinking of what you said when we parted. The precise words you used when you spoke of the future. Never once did you refer to us. Only to me. Then I realized, you were making the biggest mistake of your life. Sacrificing yourself for a monster like me."

"You wouldn't be a monster anymore, you bastard, *that's* what we paid a fucking fortune to Conleith for!"

"Changing my face doesn't change who I am. What I've done..."

"I wanted you to have a fucking chance!" Raphael exploded, snatching a rock from the ground and hurling it into the darkness. "And after this debacle they'll hunt us to the ends of the earth."

"No, they won't." Morley melted from the shadows as if they gave way for him.

Mercy had never been so conflicted to see someone in her entire life. On one hand, she was so utterly glad he had come.

On the other, she feared what he might do.

As usual, his chiseled face was cast in stone. Imperturbable. Inaccessible.

Only Pru seemed to be able to read him. To reach him.

"I'm prepared to say you were both lost in the fire," Morley offered crisply. "Consider your deaths official.

That is less paperwork for me, anyhow. But may God help you if you're caught in London again, for I won't."

Raphael turned to him, attempting to wipe some of the blood from his cheek with his sleeve. "Why do this, when our capture would be a boon?"

"Because," Morley's pale gaze snapped to Mercy, and she might have read fondness beneath the censure. "Because you were right about the boots, Detective Goode, and had I listened to you earlier, so much of this might have been avoided."

The Duchesse rejoined them, a wet cloth in her hand. She regarded the addition of the Chief Inspector with a dubious look.

Morley did little but nod, saying for her benefit, "I highly doubt the coroner will be able to determine which killed Inspector Trout. The wounds to his face or to his neck. In my opinion, he can be added to this rubbish heap of a night. I should like to avoid an international incident, besides." He gave the Duchesse a starched bow of deference.

"*Merci*," she replied.

Morley turned to gaze down at Felicity, his expression troubled to find her in the arms of one of the largest, most brutal men in Christendom. "Fainted, did she?"

Mercy nodded. "I'm afraid so." She brushed her hand over the little curls at her sister's temple, wondering if hers felt so downy soft. "Marco Villenueve terrorized her. He...he struck her."

"When we find him, I'll fucking kill him," Morley said darkly, surprising even her with his vehemence.

At that, Gabriel's neck snapped up, revealing some of his ruined lip to the torchlight.

It was Raphael who spoke, however. "I assumed he was killed in the fall down the stairs. He was a crumpled heap of bones."

Morley shook his head. "No one has been able to locate him, alas, he's quite disappeared."

A prickling at the back of Mercy's neck told her that to stand near Gabriel was possibly the most dangerous place to be at the moment.

Fury rolled off his shoulders in palpable waves.

And yet, he unfurled to stand without even jostling his burden, limping slightly as he offered Felicity into Morley's care. "It is *your* face she should see when she wakes," he said.

Morley took Felicity, eliciting a groan from the woman. "There we are. You're all right."

"You're bleeding." Mercy pointed to a pool that'd gathered where Gabriel had sat against the wall, the liquid gleaming like spilled ink in the firelight.

Gabriel only rolled his shoulder in a rather Gallic shrug, until Raphael checked the pool for himself, and found drops of blood along the path his brother had tread.

"Where are you hurt?" he demanded, clutching at his brother's coat.

"It's nothing," the man growled, reverting back to his native tongue.

"That amount of blood is not nothing, you fucking lunatic, now tell me. I'm taking you to the hospital."

"Stop fussing, little brother." Gabriel shrugged him off. "The hospital is where I'm headed anyway...it'll just be another scar."

"We'll accompany you," Raphael offered, jerking back a little when his brother held up a hand against him.

"No," he said fiercely. "I have my carriage. The plan hasn't changed, Raphael, so you must go. And if you do something impetuous and get yourself killed, I'll follow you into the afterlife and make your eternity a living hell."

"Brothers." The Duchesse made an amused sound that no one seemed to mark.

"I will meet you." Gabriel thrust a finger at his brother. "London isn't safe for you to show your face anymore."

Raphael stormed forward in protest. "But how can I—"

"*Ca suffit*, Raphael!" he snarled, causing everyone to start. *That's enough.* His enormous shoulders sagged, and he placed a hand against the wall as if he needed it to hold him up for a moment. "Just let this be easy for once. Let me not have to fight. I'm so fucking *tired* of fighting. Just...go. So I can follow. *Vive la vie.*"

Live life.

Mercy held her breath as she watched Raphael do the same, she watched the war wage within him. Love and worry for his brother, the need to survive...

Finally, he nodded. "*Vive la vie.*"

The leviathan paused for an imperceptible moment and Mercy thought his gaze might have shifted back to Felicity.

It was impossible not to have soft feelings for her sister, even for a man as hard as he.

Finally, he strode away so straight and tall, one might not even notice the drops of blood he left behind.

The shadows seemed to welcome him as one of their own, and Mercy stared into them long after his shape had disappeared.

Not because of the man who'd slid into their embrace, but because of the man behind her. The one whose embrace she craved the very most.

The one who was leaving.

Suddenly she wished the world would disappear, so she could give him a proper goodbye.

"Raphael." It was the Duchesse who said his name.

"Gabriel told me that you two have Mathilde's ashes. That you have booked tickets to take her to places that were special. Places that we—she and I—were planning to visit together."

Needing to see him, Mercy turned and found his eyes upon her even as he replied to the Duchesse. "That was...on our itinerary, yes."

She stepped forward, a proud woman unused to asking for favors. "It seems providential, don't you think, that she and I were planning on taking my ship around the world. That we were going to lose ourselves, or perhaps find ourselves in foreign ports. If you are in need of losing yourself as well...I think Mathilde would have been happy for us to keep each other company and remember her."

"Duchesse," he said carefully. "I am honored...I..."

"I think you may call me Amelie. I would prefer to put my days as a Duchesse behind me." She pulled off her mask as if freeing herself from a mantle borne too long. Flicking a coy gaze at Mercy, she said, "I will go to my little boat to have the staff ready it. We will be prepared to stop and gather anything or...anyone you may wish to take with you before we board my ship."

"*Merci*," Raphael breathed, looking a little dazed.

Above them, in the keep, Mercy was aware of an inferno eating at a piece of precious history.

And it felt like a candle compared to what burned in her bosom as she looked at him.

"This is your chance at freedom." She summoned a smile from somewhere, pasting it onto her stiff and brittle lips. "I have...much to thank you for."

She glanced to Morley, who stood looking rather uncomfortable, though whether from their conversation or the weight of the woman in his arms, it was difficult to tell.

"Well." She smoothed down her dress, soiled by the

extraordinary events of the night. "If you ever do come back to London, I can't promise I'll still be at Cresthaven. But you can find me Thursdays at the Eddard Sharpe Society. I hope you'll...that we'll...see each other."

Dammit, was she going to cry? Not in front of him. Anything but that.

Why did her heart have to choose *now* to break?

Why did saying goodbye seem like the worst thing that would ever happen to her?

Raphael reached for her, the backs of his knuckles brushing away a tear she'd not been aware had escaped.

"You look so bereft, I might weep," he murmured, his eyes crinkling with a smile that hadn't yet made it to his mouth. "It's as though you thought you were not invited along."

She blinked one. Twice. Her heart forgetting to beat as she analyzed his words.

"Are you asking me to...go? As in...with you?" Surely, she'd misheard.

"No." He stepped closer. Never had she seen such emotion in his eyes. Such unmistakable meaning. "I'm asking for so much more than that. I'm asking for *everything.*"

She drew back, pressing her hand to her forehead. "This can't be real. You were just about to—to allow yourself to be killed not an hour ago and now you're...you're...what?"

Not *proposing*, surely.

"The only reason I contemplated leaving this world, Mercy, is to save the one person who has ever loved me. I thought no reality existed where I'd get to hope for a life that could offer a woman like you." He gathered her hands, lifting each knuckle to drag beneath a worshipful kiss. "I don't want to leave this world if you're a part of it. Because you're a part of *me*, whether you love me back or not."

She choked on her own breath and spasmed in a flurry of coughs. "I'm sorry. Did you say...love?"

"I said love." He nodded, unabashedly. "I give you my heart, used and damaged as it might be. I offer you my soul, black as it is. My money, which is an obscene amount." He grinned impishly, producing that bloody dimple.

Lord, but he didn't play fair.

"My body is yours in every way. My protection. My trust." He cupped her chin in his hand, and it humiliated her to find that more tears pooled in the grooves of his palm. "I would give my life, if only for a moment beneath the sun that is your smile. Your grace. Your passion. Come with me, Mercy. Let me prove that I can deserve you."

She sniffed, so overwhelmed she felt as if she might simply float across the water like one of the gondolas. Desire so overwhelming swept her breath out of her lungs. This was what she wanted. This man. This life.

She opened her mouth as her heart sank. "I...I *can't* leave Felicity."

"Go," urged a weak voice.

She whirled to find her sister on her feet, leaning heavily on Morley, who had been astonishingly silent and stoic through the entire ordeal.

"What did you say?" Her blood was still for a full moment, while the person she held most dear looked her in the eyes with steady resolution.

And not a little bit melancholy.

"I cannot be your other half forever. You always needed more than that."

"Felicity! You can't think—"

When Mercy would have gone to her, Felicity stopped her with one gesture. "He *loves* you. And I'll be all right. I have Morley, Pru, Nora, and Titus, and it's not like you'll be gone forever. Perhaps I'll visit you in exotic places?"

Was she truly contemplating this madness? "But our parents...I can't leave you to face them in the wake of such a decision."

"I'll deal with them," Morley sighed, running an exhausted hand over his face. "Prudence will have my neck in a noose for this."

Suddenly her heart was pounding. Throbbing. Threatening to gallop away like a herd of stampeding horses.

"Surely you're not agreeing to this, Morley." She gestured at Raphael, not trusting herself to look at him. "Have you forgotten he's a thief? A ne'er-do-well? A profligate libertine I've known all of five minutes?"

"A lesser man would be wounded." Raphael placed a hand over his heart as if she'd pierced it.

"I was once all of those things." Morley stared hard at the man who offered his heart to her. "I believe we do not have to be what our circumstances would have made for us. We can forge our own path. We can choose to be better."

"All I want to be is worthy of her," Raphael said with such vehemence, she found new tears pricking at the corner of her eyes.

Morley nodded his approval. "London could be made safe for you... It would take some doing. Some time to change the narrative, to see where the balance of power shifts when all is said and done. Longueville will need seeing to. Leave that to me."

"Everyone's gone mad," Mercy realized.

Including her. Because she was actually contemplating this. Leaving her home. Her twin. Her other beloved sisters and nieces and brothers-in-law.

For the journey she'd always yearned for.

To share with a man who was beginning to mean everything to her.

Felicity drifted forward and enfolded her in an embrace, her body trembling with valiantly unshed tears. "You're miserable here, Mercy. We all know it. Our parents will return, and you'll be locked in a battle that will only end in a disastrous marriage or with you disavowed. You've always talked of independence. A grand adventure. This might be your one chance to claim it."

"What will you do? Might you come with us?" Mercy offered.

Felicity shook her head. "Mercy, for once, stop worrying about me. I'm grown, perhaps it's time I step away from your shadow. I'll toddle along. It'll be fine, just...promise me you'll write. All the time."

Mercy must have nodded, because Felicity kissed her, then turned to take Raphael's hand. "And you promise to make her happy?"

He pressed a fond kiss to her knuckles. "It's all I want, *petite sœur.*"

"She's not easy."

"I'm still right here, I'll have you know," Mercy said with no little indignation.

Raphael flashed his most charming, cocksure grin. "I'm looking forward to the challenge."

Mercy dashed away every tear, not knowing if she was infatuated or infuriated. "You're getting ahead of yourselves. I haven't even agreed to go anywhere!"

Felicity and Raphael shared a knowing smile that lit her temper. "What did I tell you?"

Raphael winked and let out a long-suffering sigh.

"Unbelievable!" Throwing up her hands, Mercy marched a few paces away, if only to try to chase her unruly emotions.

"*Mon chaton.*" Raphael caught her, and the feel of his

strong fingers threading with hers stunned her to stillness.

Not just rooting her feet to the ground but weaving something undeniable through the pads of her fingers, threading up the veins in her arm, and pouring into her heart. From there, it pulsed into the rest of her with every beat.

It was him. His name. His face.

The love that shined there when she turned back to find them alone beneath the earth.

"I can't explain it, after only knowing you such a short time," he said with the earnestness of a youth shining on the face of a brutal man who'd never been blessed with a childhood. "But I know I've always been some sort of empty vessel, and I think I understand why my entire life I've never felt whole." He pressed his hand to her heart, the palm warm as he seemed to savor what he found there. "I am not me. I am we. *Us.* That feels complete. My heart only seems to beat when you are near. I stand before you. No. I kneel at your feet."

He hit his knees, pressing his forehead to her fingers as if paying tribute to a goddess. "I am a man stripped of pride and wit. Of everything that gave me power. This is what I offer you. A new start. I'm asking —I'm begging—not for your forgiveness. Not for your mercy. But for *you.* Mercy. *For you.* Will you be mine? Will you let me call myself yours?"

She studied his face for a hint of artifice, and what she found there broke open something inside of her that exploded into incandescent sparks of the purest exhilaration. Life with this man. Discovery. Travel. Adventure. Pleasure.

Love.

Wasn't that worth any sort of risk?

A sliver of doubt dimmed his smile. "I know you

didn't want to be the property of man, Mercy. And I'd never ask that of you. You own me heart and soul, but I don't think I'd love you this passionately, if you could truly be possessed—"

"Stop." She seized him and pulled him to his feet. "Stop. I cannot take any more joy or it'll split me apart. Of course, I'm going with you. Of course, I'm yours. I was yours the moment you kissed me, you dolt. Now do it again before I change my mind."

With a smile brilliant enough to illuminate the night, he swept her in his arms and claimed her mouth, sealing their bargain with a kiss that was impossible to maintain through their unrelenting smiles.

"Come," he urged, linking his arms with hers. "Let us leave all this chaos behind."

They walked hand in hand through the shadows of the dark night, knowing that their brilliant future lay just on the other side.

EPILOGUE

*R*aphael broke through the surface of the warm waters off the Antiguan coast with a mighty surge of his limbs. The sun felt like the very smile of God on his face, and he wiped the ocean from his eyes to be greeted by a view that never ceased to strike him with pure wonder.

The gleaming white sands and the indescribably clear blue water provided the perfect backdrop for a tangle of vibrant vegetation and exotic trees. The opulent Villa de la Sol was part Spanish cathedral, part Persian palace, resplendent in the noonday brilliance.

But what made this place paradise, was the goddess draped in a hammock beneath a tasseled umbrella.

The sight of her humbled him into stillness, and Raphael treaded water, taking advantage of a rare moment to observe his wife unaware.

He woke every morning anxious to make certain he hadn't dreamed his good fortune. Mercy Goode had consented to make an honest man of him at sea—provided they omitted the part about her obeying or submitting to her husband.

When asked what word might replace the original, she'd studied him for a moment, then decided "adore."

They'd been true to their word. They loved, cherished, honored and most assuredly *adored* each other.

She nestled in a pool of thin white skirts; her bare leg draped over the side of her hammock. In her hand was *The Affair of the Benighted Bride*, the latest adventure of Detective Eddard Sharpe. The gentle ocean breeze teased locks of her unbound hair, only shades darker than the sand she kicked at with her toe, encouraging a gentle sway.

She glanced up as the Duchesse—Amelie—filled her dainty glass with a juice made from the local guava fruit she'd mixed with champagne.

The women toasted each other, and Amelie must have said something witty because Mercy tossed her curls back, exposing her elegant throat as she laughed with unrestricted abandon.

A wave of joy threatened to drown him.

Christ, he worshiped her with such uninhibited devotion, he became jealous of the sun's own caress on her skin.

Raphael disrupted a school of tiny, colorful fish as he displaced the water with powerful strokes. He swam until he could use his feet against the sand to propel him through a tide that tried its utmost to hinder his advance.

By the time he'd reached the beach upon which the women reclined, the two were locked in an animated discussion, gesturing wildly.

"... And that is why women belong on the bench and in juries." She waved her book. "J. Francis Morgan is plainly saying that surely such a gross miscarriage of justice would not have occurred should a woman have had ought to do with the case. She would have seen through the ruse right away. Why must it be a man's world when they do a right proper job of cocking it up?"

Raphael kept wisely silent on the subject as he made his approach.

Amelie wrapped her arms around her bent legs and rested her chin on her knees. "Women know that it isn't a man's world. Not completely. We simply have a more subtle influence. We change things when men are not looking, thinking they are important to play at war and conquest."

"But they do more damage than we can repair," Mercy said with vicious passion. "I don't want my influence to be subtle. I want to change things while they watch. While they weep."

"I've no doubt you will." Raphael retrieved a towel from the small stand he'd driven into the sand, upon which his clothing hung.

"You, my love, are merciless."

"And *you* are not the first person to tell me that."

As he applied the towel to his skin, Amelie finished her drink in two impressive swallows and pushed to her feet. "If you will excuse me, those of us with red in our hair are wise to get out of the sun after noonday," she said with a languorous stretch. "Besides, I need to pack if we are to leave for the States, where we will no longer be allowed to lounge about in the half-nude, more is the pity."

She flashed them both a cheeky wink before lifting a hem that had been cut like a riding kit. Flowing and feminine, but certainly more trouser than skirt.

Raphael bid her adieu before draping the towel over his head and scrubbing as much of the ocean water from his scalp as he could.

"For a life on the lam, I say we're surviving rather well," he remarked before drying his face and neck.

"I dare say I'm enjoying my time as an exile," his wife replied blithely. "And I certainly have no complaints regarding the view."

He surfaced from beneath the towel to find her eyes making a lazy, appreciative journey up his torso.

His body responded to the heat in her gaze, though he decided to allow her a respite as she'd declined to join him in the water due to the arrival of her monthly courses and complaints of fatigue.

Still, he joined her on the hammock, his weight forcing her to roll toward him, allowing him to gather her close and fuse their mouths for a deep kiss that tasted of passion, guava, and a hint of brine.

"Tell me, wife, about what sparked your indignance at your novel?"

She opened her mouth, then closed it with a befuddled expression. "I'll have to reread the passage now. You've made it quite impossible to pay attention."

He drew a finger down the line of her nose. "I'm learning your attention is often difficult to pin down."

She turned her head to the side, playfully avoiding his next kiss. "That's ridiculous. You don't know the first thing about—" She seized his bicep. "Raphael. *Look.* There's a dolphin!" Pointing in her excitement, she leaned so far forward, the hammock would have been unsettled had he not been there to steady it. "An entire family of them. Oh! I've never seen such a thing."

He draped her across his chest, his amusement at her overwrought delight spilling over as laughter.

He decided to forgo taunting her with an *I told you so.*

They settled back to sway, and watched gleaming grey sea creatures frolic and leap, seeming to mimic their joy.

Lingering long after the dolphins disappeared, Raphael coiled one of her curls around his finger, enjoying the waves, the breeze, and the closeness between them.

"I don't think I've ever been happier than this moment," he murmured, pressing his lips to her temple. "I wish I could bottle this feeling like a scent. That I could wear it on my skin always. Escape back here whenever life is bleak."

She pushed up, bracing her hands on his chest as she leveled him a sober look. "You know, the more I love you, the angrier I am with you. To think that you almost missed this. That you might have died..."

"I concocted that scheme before I met you because I'd never truly felt alive." He dropped his forehead against hers. "You changed all that."

Her lip quirked. "I suppose I'll have to forgive you eventually."

"You could punish me first, if you like," he suggested with a naughty wink. "A hundred tongue lashings. Or real lashings, if that's what you prefer."

She gave him a half-hearted shove before settling down against him once more. "I'm excited for the life we're going to live together, and I'm happy to see America, though I'm not looking forward to donning my corset again."

He chuffed, before a familiar anxiety lanced through him. "Do you ever get homesick for England?"

Staring into the distance, she replied, "I miss my sisters. I worry for Felicity. But I know we'll go back, eventually. I'm in no great hurry."

He caught her hand. "We'll go back. We'll go anywhere you are happy," he vowed.

She caught both of his wrists and pulled them around her. "I'm happy right here. In your arms. I can miss England sometimes, but I'm incapable of being homesick."

"Oh?" His lips found the shell of her ear and stopped for a nibble. "Why is that?"

"Because, husband, my home is wherever you are."

ALSO BY KERRIGAN BYRNE

A GOODE GIRLS ROMANCE
Seducing a Stranger
Courting Trouble
Dancing With Danger
Tempting Fate
The Earl of Christmas Past

THE BUSINESS OF BLOOD SERIES
The Business of Blood
A Treacherous Trade
A Vocation of Violence

VICTORIAN REBELS
The Highwayman
The Hunter
The Highlander
The Duke
The Scot Beds His Wife
The Duke With the Dragon Tattoo

THE MACLAUCHLAN BERSERKERS
Highland Secret
Highland Shadow
Highland Stranger
To Seduce a Highlander

THE MACKAY BANSHEES

ABOUT THE AUTHOR

 Kerrigan Byrne is the USA Today Bestselling and award winning author of THE DUKE WITH THE DRAGON TATTOO. She has authored a dozen novels in both the romance and mystery genre. Her newest mystery release THE BUSINESS OF BLOOD is available October 24th, 2019

She lives on the Olympic Peninsula in Washington with her dream boat husband. When she's not writing and researching, you'll find her on the water sailing and kayaking, or on land eating, drinking, shopping, and taking the dogs to play on the beach.

Kerrigan loves to hear from her readers! To contact her or learn more about her books, please visit her site: www.kerriganbyrne.com